DREAMMARE

Harvey Price

Publisher: Harvey L. Price, Jr.
Madras, Oregon

ISBN: 978-0-9819220-6-5

Library of Congress Control Number: 2010910398

Back and Front Cover: Used with Permission from Tom Hall, Technical Director/Owner of Sleep Disorders of Palm Springs, Palm Springs, California.

Printed by Minuteman Press, Olympia, Washington and bound by Phil's Bindery, Seattle, Washington.

FOR

Zelma, Alfred William, Harriet
and Harvey Sr.

Also Written by Harvey Price

THE LAST ARK

SPEAK!

FETCH! (THE JOURNEY CONTINUES)

THE RETRIEVER

DON'T ROCK THE BOAT!

ACCREDITATION TIME

ACKNOWLEDGEMENT

Probably most of what is contained in this story can be traced back over the years to those who I studied under, was influenced by or worked with in theological training or in health care. The most memorable of these individuals were Sterling, Alexander, Albert, Mary, Priscilla, Bob, Hal, Bill, Victor, Lance, Patricia, Eileen, John, Glen, Pete, Frank, Jan, Roger, Charlene, Susan, Kay, Barbara, Idora, Kerry, Tom, Linda, Lynn, Diana, Leslie, Debbie, Fred and Tom.

Each in their own way instructed, inspired, tolerated and forgave me enough that I was able to keep going forward. The dedication to their vocations has touched countless individuals across this world. And each of them remains a great source of wonder to me.

And to Jeannie, Tom, Elizabeth, Jeanne, Renae and the other Tom, thank you again and again.

FOREWORD

It will soon become obvious that this book is a darker tale; one in which the world is held hostage after being subjected to unmerciful cruelty and destruction. Take heart, however, because each of us can still ensure that there is a new dawn by making wiser choices involving consuming less, giving back more and worshipping faithfully. But never forgetting, all the while, we must still be ever vigilant as to the content of our dreams and of any darkened strangers who might suddenly appear uninvited into them.

THE FIRST NIGHT

ONE: THE SETTING

Before anyone realized there was such a concept as time, space or volume, there was at least sleep. It was probably the first significant phenomena or dimension that the earliest humanoids, anywhere, identified and analyzed. From that, the other properties which define the reality around us were conceptualized and incorporated into our daily lives. But sleep has remained the least understood and most mythologized of all that exists naturally.

So puzzling, in fact, was dreaming, that most worrisome, feared and inspiring portion of sleep, that shamans, soothsayers, mystics and noblemen began to attach great significance to its content. Much later, when it was possible to record the contents and analyses surrounding dreams and dreaming, volumes began to be written about them. It was then their significance in a person's daily life became even more prominent.

And so it went. Sleep analysis and dreamtime interpretation became a legitimate scientific discipline and their importance in the health of an individual was unquestioned. And despite the abnormalities that were seen, diagnosed and treated…some successfully and others not as consistently so, all the phenomena or stages of sleep remained confined or isolated within or immediately associated with each individual's body.   In other words, nothing left their body during sleep, aside from rhythmical snoring and occasionally other sounds or possibly some bodily fluids.   Everything was naturally occurring, and it all could be directly and rationally linked back to sleep.   It became a tidy, scientific phenomenon to study.

Until that one night.

As is so often the case when someone has a terrifying event to hurriedly and secretly document as I have, the reporter, or in this case the principle witness, has a rather lengthy but usually a fairly indistinct memory of its beginnings.   That is absolutely not the case now.   Nothing led up to its beginning.   Nothing indicated that anything was amiss with any equipment, the patient or the findings thus far in the testing process.   It was as routine a night as I could have ever hoped for.   Until it all began.

I must now somehow report what I have seen and heard that first night and the others that followed, as well as the weeks thereafter.   Who knows who may be left to read it… or even want to?   Or know how.   The terror spread so rapidly.   Why I was apparently the first to witness its beginning, I'll never know.   And why I am immune to its full-blown appearance, at least up until this point, or from the same fate as has befallen so many others, I'll never really understand.   I am too afraid at this point to analyze anything.   All I can or want to do now is make this record and hope to God that someday, someone will read it.   I fear that time is running out… for everyone.   For now, "they" are gone, but no one knows when or if they might return.

That first night began without incident.   I arrived at

the hospital my usual time, around 7 p.m. The first patient would arrive at 8 p.m.; and the second, my last one, would come to the sleep laboratory at 9 p.m. The overall plan was to have both patients briefed, prepared, with all the electrodes attached, the equipment calibrated and each one ready for sleep by 10:00 p.m. From then, the plan was for them to sleep naturally for the next four hours. During that period their brain waves; eye, chest, abdominal and leg movements; air exchange in and out of their airways; heart rhythms; oxygen saturation levels and body positions would be monitored on a fourteen channel polysomnograph.

If, at the end of that period of time, there were significant enough abnormalities noted that could possibly be treated, the second phase of the study would be instituted. There were some patients who were not scheduled for this type of study, and they would be allowed to simply sleep the entire night away without having to be awakened for a particular treatment modality. But they were a small minority. 80% of the patients seen in the laboratory I worked in had the split-night study, in other words, a diagnostic work-up at the beginning and some form of treatment the latter half of the night. And somewhere between 5 and 6 a.m. each patient would be awakened, disconnected and allowed to go home.

For the sake of preparing anyone who might read this report, I must include in this summary of the laboratory work site its particular location and surroundings. It has some bearing on how what was to begin happening affected me.

The lab was located in the basement of a large medical office building. However, in addition to the usual physician offices and clinical laboratories, there was a large outpatient surgical section, which incorporated most of the first floor. The second and third floors were comprised of physician offices, reception areas and exam rooms. The basement, where I worked, remained largely unused; it was essentially unfinished. It awaited an occupant who was willing to invest a considerable amount of money to enclose and decorate the unused area. Our laboratory abutted this expansive, and to me, a mostly desolate area. At night, its hollowness served as an echo chamber for any sounds that occurred in the hallways or adjoining rooms. And truly important for my upcoming experience of isolation and terror, by 6 p.m. there were no other employees or outpatients and their families in or around the building. I was the only person in this massive building until my first patient for the evening arrived.

And their coming into this setting was obviously somewhat unnerving for them as well. I had to spend the first few minutes of my introduction attempting to put them at ease and orienting them as to what the night's study would entail. It was important to establish the necessary trust and rapport with these patients as soon as possible. The success of the study depended on them feeling becalmed and as relaxed as possible.

On this one particular night, I felt that I had been successful with each patient in achieving their cooperation and putting them fully at ease with what would happen throughout the night. Oddly enough, neither individual was to have the split study. Each one would be allowed to sleep undisturbed through the night. In other words, I would not be waking them for the treatment phase. And in that regard, I was looking forward to a rather easy night's work. The main problem with such a workload was staying alert. By not having to get up and interrupt the patient's sleep, I was left with simply noting their behavior and their physiological parameters each hour, as well as commenting on our work sheets any unusual behaviors and requests. Often, around 1-2 a.m., the urge for me to doze became rather intense. To fight it, I would walk in circles or jog in place. I couldn't just sit at the computer console and stare at the flowing stream of data and not be hypnotized to the point that my eyes began to close. And I wasn't alone in that regard. It was an occupational hazard. Each of us who tested and treated the patients in this environment had to fight this natural tendency.

After all, night is for sleeping... even for those of us who are testing sleeping subjects. Nighttime sleep is also the period when our mind sorts out what happened throughout the just-completed day. It replays old fears and fantasies, recognizes and recharges the body and brain for another day's labor and now, most significant of all, it has eventually and tragically become the avenue for the most frightful emergence in all of human history.

Always grateful that both hook-ups of the myriad leads and other attachments had been successfully calibrated, that each computer screen was now delivering interference-free data for storage of every single breath, brainwave and heartbeat, and that the audio and visual connections were working and a clear infrared camera picture was streaming from each room, I breathed a sigh of relief. I already sensed this night was going to be less hectic and challenging. I could let my guard down, and just focus on doing my hourly notations on the patients' logs for the morning staff that would download, analyze the data and then give it to our Medical Director to interpret the next day.

And it was always at this very moment that I took my first deep breath and would become aware of the quiet and absolute solitude of my work station. It was as if there was no one else anywhere, other than the two study subjects seen on the video monitors, which were positioned above each computer screen. They displayed rather hazy outlines of them in their respective beds. As my focus intensified, my awareness of the world outside this laboratory diminished progressively, as if we were an island floating somewhere amidst the stars. Darkness enveloped us. The only sounds were became those of progressively deeper and rhythmic breathing, occasional sighs, rustling of bed covers and the uninterrupted hum of the computers and other electronic equipment at their bedsides and located in front of me. It was a soothing, computer-age symphony; a nighttime lullaby. It lulled you, and on this first night of what was to become only the first of an endless series of shocks and horror, it beguiled me into a state of innocent inattentiveness.

TWO: THE FIRST STUDY

I was always relieved when my calibrations for both of my study patients went smoothly, without my having to reposition or refresh the electrode contacts.   Interference, whether from poor electrode contact or placement; the patient being cold or nervous or from all the external equipment needed to perform these studies, is the bane of anyone doing these types of studies.   And on this particular night, my set-ups went smoothly and produced a flawless tracing of all seventeen channels for both patients.

This is important for you to know, because it was later during one of these same studies that a mysterious probe seeking an entry portal occurred.   And naturally, at the time, I was convinced it was some kind of interference; a power surge or a transformer malfunction somewhere in the neighborhood.   Coincidentally, there was a forecast for storms in the area sometime that same night.   I was convinced, or at least that is what I told myself over and over, that what occurred was an externally caused event. Nothing, not anything ever imaginable, could have convinced me or even crossed my mind that it might be internal or organic to the patient.

But, probably before I go too much further and

without my having to go into too much detail, you should have some idea how a typical sleep study progresses. Doing so will help calm me somewhat in the retelling and give anyone reading this an idea of how unusual and eventually terrifying what I was to witness really was.

To begin with, sleep is divided into four stages. Three of them, N1, 2 and 3 are associated with Non-rapid Eye Movement or NREM sleep. In these stages there is usually little memorable dreaming. However, during the N1 stage, which is considered the transition time from being awake, when alpha brainwaves transition to theta waves, there can occur what's called hypnologic hallucinations. These alone can be startling and frightening in themselves. That's because you have lost some muscle tone during this initial sleep phase and these "dreamlets", as I call them, can initiate a "flight or fight" response. They are common in people who suffer from narcolepsy. Likewise, during this phase there can be muscle jerking or twitching as well. Awareness of events or conditions around you is lessened considerably as you enter this first stage.

N2 stage is characterized by the initial appearance of sleep spindles and/or K-complexes. Spindles are runs of the most rapid frequency of electrical activity seen during sleep, and K-complexes are the largest of the electrical complexes seen; but in their case they are isolated and are unmistakable. During this stage the patient or any individual's awareness of any external activity or conditions disappears. This stage comprises anywhere from 45% to 55% of the total sleep in adults having a normal night's sleep.

N3 stage is considered deep sleep, in which at least 20% of brainwave activity is comprised of delta waves or a long series of large complexes. It is in this stage that someone may experience night terrors, sleep-talking, bedwetting or I could note an individual attempting to sleepwalk. This is not a stage of sleep that I will see too much of if someone is suffering from a moderate to severe sleep disorder. Their sleep patterns are too disrupted for them to progress into deep slumber. However, if we need to perform the treatment portion of a sleep study, which as I mentioned I was not doing on this particular night, the patient may not have any Stage N3 sleep for the first four hours of the study; but with successful treatment he or she may rapidly descend into it as their body can achieve a measure of homeostasis and well-being. Invariable, if this is achieved during the study, they awaken feeling more refreshed and alert than they have been in months or years, depending on their medical history. Normally, this stage of sleep accounts for anywhere from 20% to 30% of total sleep time, depending on the person's health and how much N1 sleep they have.

Finally, the fourth stage is REM or Rapid Eye Movement sleep. And in normal adults it might account for 20%-25% of total sleep time. What distinguishes this stage of sleep is the presence of rapid eye movement. (*See LEOG and REOG, the eye channels, on DREAMMARE's book cover.*) This stage is associated with low voltage or much smaller brainwaves than those seen in stage N3. In addition, there is usually an accompanying loss of muscle tone; some clinicians even describing it as a type of paralysis. And it is in this stage that vivid dreaming occurs.

But I must pause here and expand further on this stage of sleep, because it is in this stage where this chilling account begins. It was to signal the ultimate threat to all human life.

There are anywhere from three to five cycles of the

above mentioned stages, depending on the age and health of an individual. Characteristically, each cycle ends with REM stage; and each of those episodes of REM become longer as the night's sleep progresses. But because of the strange circumstances and particularly unique protocol associated with having a sleep study, these episodes of REM seen in our clinic can be shorter and fewer, with the final one occurring sometime between 3 a.m. and 5 a.m. And in the case of the two patients I was seeing this particular night, I fully expected their final and longest REM stage would be around 30 minutes. There are and were certainly exceptions, given the lab's setting and the patient's ability to accommodate to wearing the necessary monitoring equipment. It seemed almost each night offered some surprise, and this one was certainly no different in that respect.

With the laboratory's bedroom lights turned out and their infrared cameras turned on in each patient room, I settled down into the absolute quiet of the monitoring room. Aside from the purring of the computers, the other sounds were those of the patients' settling in their beds and their breathing becoming more regular. There was a kind of rhythmic and eclectic symphonic quality to it all. The computer's hum comprised the string section, the patients' breathing sounds were the woodwinds, and their louder outbursts of coughing, wheezing or snoring were the percussion section. The stage was set and with the types of patients I was seeing this night, I expected these studies to pass peacefully and uneventfully until daybreak.

But I was wrong. Something quite unusual did occur. And it was almost as if it was purposefully trying to get my attention. By that I mean, I wasn't too sure whether the incident had repeated itself numerous times before I finally recognized it happening. And then once I did, there were no reoccurrences. Anyway, my first realization of some strange and mystifying artifact was when the patient in Room 1 entered her final REM stage for the night. I later noted in my technologist notes that it occurred at 4:30 a.m.

There was nothing odd, aside from its presence, which caught my attention when it did occur. The equipment had performed perfectly before and after its sudden appearance. Nothing led up to its occurrence or followed it. There were no unfamiliar noises, no patient movement seen on the infrared image nor was there any telltale twitching or muscle artifact from the limb leads. The patient was perfectly still, as a result of her being in mid-REM sleep.

What caught my attention was the sudden appearance of a solid black spot in the space between the two eye leads on the computer-generated recording. It was like a drop of black ink had mysteriously dropped onto some paperwork on an office desk. Or, more specifically, as I later thought about it, it was like a stain on someone's clothing. It appeared to have a permanent quality about it. There was nothing transitory, like an electrical artifact; it was devoid of all reflective properties. It almost had a strange, depth-like quality to it; like an unknown dimension of some kind. Once I did notice it, it did not reappear. There was just that one time: the spot. So before I could get up out of my wheeled armchair to check on the equipment and electrode attachments, it was gone and did not reappear. As I said before, I was sure it was interference of some kind, something external to the lab. I made no note of its occurrence in my paperwork. It seemed meaningless.

That same patient did report on her post-test questionnaire, which allows the patient to evaluate and comment on the night's study and care provided by me that she awoke with a severe headache. And upon my questioning her further whether that was a common occurrence for her, she answered that it was not. She could never remember having one after a night's sleep before. Even more puzzling, she appeared to stagger somewhat after my equipment was disconnected and as she began to walk out of the laboratory once dressed. I had to steady her. She acknowledged at the time that she was a little dizzy, but refused my offer to observe her longer in the clinic until she was sure it had passed.

It wasn't until a couple of days later that Tom, my supervisor, asked me if I had seen the notice in the morning newspaper that this same patient had died sometime after her sleep study and that her funeral was that day. There was no cause of death noted in the obituary. He added that the tone of the obituary was that all family and friends were shocked at the suddenness of her passing.

And it wasn't until even later that I had time to review her study, after it had been downloaded onto a CD and I could scan the course of her entire sleep study. I got out her folder and noted the time of the anomaly in my notes and scanned to that timeframe. And to emphasize once again, these computer-recorded studies account for every event, every breath, heartbeat and the slightest movement of the patient throughout the night. And when I streamed the computer cursor to 4:30 a.m., the page was absolutely clear! There was no solid black stain. There was no record of any of the seventeen channels on that page. It was blank for that sixty second interval.

THE PROGESSION

THREE: NIGHT TWO

This missing data confused and concerned me.
Primarily, my concern was that I may have caused this
full-page disappearance.   Somehow I must have made a
technical error when manipulating the incoming data.   I
reviewed over and over in my mind what happened and was
sure that I hadn't hit any computer keys that might have
deleted anything.   Likewise, nothing had been turned off or
removed the entire night.   The patient, as I recalled, never
even called out to have a restroom break.   It was, as far as I
could tell, a flawless study, aside from that one episode of
interference.   And yet, now that page was completely
missing from the study.   I was more confused than ever
after reviewing these circumstances.

Inquiring how this might have happened with Tom
and Dr. Hildreth, our Medical Director, neither had any
answer that fit the occasion.   It left them both puzzled as
well.   Nothing preceded the empty space nor did there
appear to be any electronic malfunction afterwards.   It was
simply this one page that was absent of any clinical data.
Shrugging our shoulders, we decided to just let the matter

rest.   Computers, we each acknowledged, in this line of work, they were totally unpredictable.

And as it happened, I didn't have another night with someone simply having an all night study, one not needing any treatment phase, until five days later.   But on this night, my other patient for that night did have a split-night study. This meant that I would be spending some dedicated time with that patient and not be fully focused on the two computer monitors all night.   But that was rarely an issue. These patients were sleeping… after all.   And again on this night, both hook-ups went smoothly and there was no interference or need to reapply any electrodes.

In fact, most of the night passed quickly and without incident.   I was able to quickly select and determine which device the second patient would use for his treatment; and he immediately fell deep asleep, rebounding into stages N3 and REM sleep for the remainder of his study.   The first patient continued to cycle through the four stages of sleep and was experiencing a good twenty minute REM episode when I looked at the office wall clock and noticed that it was 4:30 a.m.   Casually, I glanced over at her monitor; and to my shock and surprise, the same blotch appeared, again wedged in between the two eye channels.   And this time it appeared larger and had the distinct appearance of some depth of field, like it was alternating in and out of a three-dimensional shape.   Almost like it was breathing!   Resisting the impulse to become too startled, I stared closer, and saw that it indeed appeared to be shrinking and then expanding.   But it only appeared to be doing this during this same sixty second timeframe.   In the follow-up screen, it was gone, which prevented me from capturing it by printing out a sheet.   And I didn't feel comfortable at that time to leave the streaming data and trace back to that screen.   Something more could happen if I left the real-time acquisition, and I might miss an even more important finding or artifact.

All this left me even more puzzled and now more than mildly worried. Was someone tapping into our laboratory? Was this a new kind of computer virus, impervious to our antivirus software or malware? Immediately, I looked up at the video display of the patient and noted that there was nothing amiss as far as I could see. Wanting to confirm that she was ok, I got up and quietly opened the door into her bedroom and checked the premises with my flashlight. There was nothing noteworthy. Her breathing was regular, heart rate normal, and she continued on in REM sleep. I would have to wait until morning to scan her entire study and review what I had seen. Though I tried not to, I was becoming progressively more concerned. It didn't seem to have anything to do with my technique. It appeared to happen totally apart from anything mechanical or electrical in the room. But I could only assume it was an externally caused artifact; anything else was unimaginable.

However, a chill did creep into my consciousness. For the first time I felt alone in the lab, even though there were two patients fast asleep in its safety net. Each night we always lock the outside door into the public hallway. This is done after the last patient arrives. Given the tendency of vagrants looking for a place to sleep or for those who seek to ransack medical offices, our laboratory offered a convenient shelter or a likely target. It was not uncommon for me to hear someone twisting our outside doorknob during the night. However, for some unexplainable reason, that door being locked and the two patients still tucked away in their beds did not comfort me. As farfetched as it seemed, I sensed something or someone else was probing, as if seeking entrance into our laboratory by whatever means possible.

And because this was my last work night for the week, once I had disconnected and bid the evening's patients a good day, I decided to catch a nap before the day shift came in and then review this last study with Tom again. His experience and expertise with computers and years of reading sleep studies far exceeded mine He had an objectivity and down-to-earth sensibility about him that gave me confidence that even this persistent variant could be explained and dismissed.

Steadying myself somewhat, I was eventually able to drift into a light sleep around 6:30 a.m. I knew that Tom usually arrived around 8:00 a.m. for the day shift. At least I could doze and calm down somewhat before he arrived.

I awoke when I heard him rustling about within our office, filling the coffee machine and turning on the radio for the morning news. It was a daily ritual for him. Being sleep deprived myself, I had to be careful getting up too suddenly. My equilibrium was not in top form these mornings after I finished my four night's of work.

Sitting on the edge of the bed, I thought that it always amazes me, or probably more truthfully, saddens and angers me that people like me who work odd hours, all night, on call or around the clock to provide medical and emergency services or guard our shores and keep us safe in our homes will only earn twenty to thirty dollars an hour, while there are sports figures, politicians and entertainers who so often fritter away their lavish millions, while endlessly telling us how much they are worth it all.   I know for a fact that there are lawyers who, at a minimum, charge you $195.00 for any portion of an hour they listen and question you; and then it can become upwards of $500.00 an hour if they have to go to court for you.   And what risk is there for any of these folks?

What sacrifice? What danger? The most I've ever made was $24.00 an hour.

I'm convinced, even in the sleepless stupor I was in that morning, that until discrepancies like these are addressed, our country, which should have been the grandest beacon to all the world, is in its final moments.

I admit, at that moment, I was exhausted and desperately needed more sleep, but I still needed to talk to Tom. Something strange was happening, and I needed to know if others were experiencing it or whether it was only happening during my studies.

Opening the bedroom door that faced our office area, I called out, "Yo, Tom, I need to speak with you before the onrush of a busy Friday starts and before Dr. Hildreth arrives."

"What's up?!" he asked, startled by my sudden and rare appearance in this manner.

By the end of our fourth night's work, all of us yearned to head home for the three days' rest and recovery that we so desperately needed after being sleep deprived for the last four nights. It was a hallowed ritual: flee the lab, letting nothing delay you after that last study night. Only rarely did I ever stay back to discuss something with Dr. Hildreth or Tom.

"I had another one of those strange episodes last night when the patient was in her last cycle of REM sleep and the same, unusual artifact appeared that I told you about five days ago. And again it only occurred during a sixty second time span, and then it was gone. But something else occurred that concerned me at the time."

"What was that?" he rather impatiently muttered, indicating that my presence was not particularly helping him get his customary start of the day.

He, like the rest of us, is dependent on habitual behavior and sequences to the day and week. It makes the work load easier. You can deal with the surprises and emergencies easier if part of your day is automatic and predictable. If everything that happens during a given day is a variant or surprise, you become exhausted and are prone to make mistakes. If there are numerous other staff members and colleagues interacting with you, then there are checks and balances in busier areas of a medical center or critical job site. But for us who work in isolated areas or with few associates around us, keeping your mental edge is vital. And a predictable routine helps maintain it. I was interrupting Tom's routine.

"The artifact or object appeared to shrink and expand, like it was vibrating or breathing. It gave me a sense of it having depth, of not being just a stain on the screen."

"Which patient was it?" he sighed.

"The individual in Room One," I answered quickly. "And it occurred at around the same time the first of these strange interruptions occurred five days ago. I think it was around 4:30 a.m."

"Ok. Let me get your folder on the patient and download the study onto a CD to review. I don't want to tamper with the original study. We can just examine the study on an extra CD and then destroy it afterwards, if we need to."

There then followed a flourish of activity, which only Tom could perform with the array of computers that were lined up on our work counter. He had an uncanny ability to trouble-shoot any problem they created, all of which seemed endless and unfathomable to me. He was like an orchestra conductor, once he sat down in front of them and began sorting out the data and problems that the previous night's studies had created. Between him and Dr. Hildreth, this lab was tops in the region. And that was the reason I wanted to get to the bottom of what this artifact was all about. I didn't want it to somehow contaminate the test results. I worried the timeframe of its presence could increase, likely destroying valuable data captured by these studies.

Soon he sat down in front of the computer screen that I used for the particular patient whose study I was concerned about, and slid a CD into its mainframe's slot. And within a couple of minutes of moving the computer mouse and typing in some instructions the study was transferred onto the CD and was now being relayed back onto the same computer for us to examine. Within a few minutes Tom had then quickly advanced the record to 4:25 a.m. and then stopped and began a minute-by-minute frame progression to 4:30. And once at that point, to both our amazement, this page was completely blank.

"See!" I blurted out, "It happened again! There is no test data. It's blank again for the exact period of time when I observed this artifact. It erases the patient's record. Could it be some malware or virus? But why at the exact moment and in the exact manner as before?"

"I can't say," Tom answered, obviously becoming equally puzzled and worried about what ramifications this could have for the entire laboratory. "We need to try and get a clear picture of what you are seeing. We need a hard copy of what you see before the page goes blank. In the meantime, I'm going to defrag the computer and run a thorough virus check. Was this the same computer you used when this anomaly occurred the first time?"

"No it isn't," I replied. "It was the one next to it."

"That's even more worrisome. We've got to try and scrub all the computers of any contamination and then alert everyone to print out a copy of any strange-appearing artifact immediately after it occurs, at any time throughout the study, especially if it occurs around 4:30 a.m. My hope after cleaning the hard drives is that we won't see this happen again. Thanks for bringing it to my attention. Now go home and get some needed rest. I'll see you next week."

His resolve and reassurance gave me the comfort that I needed. And after a good nap for the rest of that morning, I was able to forget about what had happened and enjoyed the next three days off. They were to be my last such carefree days. Looking back on them now, they seem to have belonged to someone else.

FOUR: NIGHT THREE

Adding to my false sense of reassurance that what I had been seeing was unimportant, Tom told me that next week all the computers desperately needed to be scrubbed of extraneous files, studies and "ejunk", as he called it. He was convinced that this maintenance work would eliminate the possibility of any other strange appearances and disappearances of artifact and data. And so it was for my first night back to work. But as I looked back, it was also a night when both patients had the "split-night" studies, each requiring a treatment. However, even with that being the case, I was thoroughly lulled into believing that our little problem was over.

But before I get too much further into the actual incident of the following night, I need to give you some background on our use and quality of the images displayed on our video monitors above each study computer in the laboratory. Surprisingly, the infrared camera, while being almost completely unobtrusive, does provide a rather detailed, live picture of what is happening immediately around the patient's bed and any activity that might occur in the bed. We can easily distinguish body position, even though the computer does have an electrode that gives us that information, as well as any patient movement. For instance, if they attempt to sit up, stand or thrash about, we can document that. But we cannot see facial expressions, and we cannot distinguish any other images in sharp focus. There is little depth of field, in other words. The images are blurred, but still are helpful and provide additional safety for the patient.

Now, I must try and describe to you what happened next during my second night after Tom worked on our computers... as hard as it is for me right now to revisit the horror of it all. Still, you need to know that on this particular night I again had two all night, uninterrupted studies, those that did not require any treatment. This meant, more importantly for what happened later in the night, I would not be diverted away from the office where our computers are monitoring and recording the two studies. In other words, I do not have to go into either room all night, unless I am called to unhook someone for them to go to the restroom. And on this night there were two gentlemen being studied.

Fortunately, again, their hook-ups and calibration procedures went smoothly and both individuals were fast asleep within ten minutes of my turning off the lights in their rooms. But, as mentioned before, I was still left with the infrared cameras monitoring their rooms. The fisheye lens gave me a fairly good panorama of the rooms' interiors, with each bed, of course, being the central focus.

Remembering the last two nights that I had an all-night sleeper, not needing treatment, I naturally became a little hesitant around 4 a.m. And for some reason, despite it being only my second work night for the week, I was becoming groggier about that time. I had to force myself to stay awake and to do the hourly log checks, which always included my verifying the patient's position in bed by looking at the video monitor for each room.

It's important for you to understand that by this time in the night the overall atmosphere inside the laboratory is quite other-worldly. There are no sounds, other than from the electronic equipment and occasionally some patient movement or snoring. This silence can be both reassuring and disquieting, depending on one's level of fatigue and alertness. For me, besides my being less alert, I was on edge. Something did not seem right; even though this entire night's hourly worksheet that we check off for each patient was uneventful and normal. I was done checking each patient by 4:20 a.m. But I was becoming progressively more nervous for some unknown reason. If I could have thought more clearly at the time, I would have been able to describe it as fear. I didn't want to be alone at that moment. Something was terribly wrong, and it had nothing to do with our equipment or the patients. There was almost an odor of danger seeping into the darkened laboratory.

I got up and walked out into the hallway which passed by each patient's room. I checked that I had securely locked the front door. I checked the restroom to make sure no one was somehow in there. I checked Dr. Hildreth's office and the third sleep lab room that was not being used this night. But nothing was amiss, and that only increased my apprehension. Not counting the two study patients, I sensed that I was not alone.

Slipping back into the office, I sat back down and did a quick check on the first room's patient. Both his video image and the computer recording were normal. Then at 4:30 a.m. I checked the second patient's computer screen and there, pulsating as if taking heaving breaths, were a series of larger and larger stains, imbedded in between the two eye channels. There was not the one blackened area this time. There was a series of them, coursing across the screen in front of me!

Terrified at what I was seeing unfold before me, I then glanced up at the video monitor and saw the patient lying undisturbed on his right side, but at the foot of his bed was a large, ill-defined shadow. It was swaying from side to side. And the shadow was not being cast from some piece of furniture or a fixture. It was moving, and it was obviously alive!

Immediately, the isolation and loneliness of where I was began sweeping through me. I became completely paralyzed and thought my bowels were going to expel all their contents. My breathing became shallow and my heart felt like it was going to surge right through my chest wall; it was beating so hard and fast. I wanted to scream for help. I wanted to flee that place. Somewhere… deep inside me, I knew what I was seeing was responsible for what had been occurring over the last nine days, even though I had no idea as of that moment who or what it was. Those spots were a prelude to this sighting. There was a stranger in this lab, and it had powers far beyond anything imaginable. And I had nowhere to run. Duty compelled me to stay in place. But in those first moments, all I could do was sit there paralyzed and stare, first at the computer screen and then with all the dread anyone could imagine, at the video monitor.

Before I could regain any control of my run-away emotions and reactions to this intrusion, the shadowy image had disappeared from view. And the stain on the computer screen was also gone. But now I became dreadfully aware of something behind me. And the same odor that I imagined previously now filled our office area; it confirmed that I was not alone. In response to this realization, I simply bowed my head and tried desperately to regain some control over my emotions and bodily reactions. For the sake of my patients lying so helplessly in their rooms, I had to regain some composure. My safety had to become secondary, but I didn't know if I could be so bold or brave. Nothing in my life thus far had prepared me for this moment.

Forcing myself to break away from staring at the computer and video screens, I slowly inched my gaze down toward the worktable and then onto the computer keyboard in front of me. I gradually began to sweep around turning my entire upper body, as if I was on a pivot and my lower body was paralyzed. Being in an armchair, with its arms abutting the counter top, I felt like I was imprisoned at that moment. It allowed me no means of escape. All I could do was force myself to face this unimaginable intruder that had been repeatedly probing our laboratory by some unearthly means. Our laboratory was in its usual lockdown and completely isolated from the outside world… this world… but not from the one that whatever was behind me came from..

Gradually and filled with the most intense fear I'd ever known, I began to see the edge of something that appeared to swallow all light, it was so black. It was at the very edge of my left eye's peripheral vision. And as I continued to turn, more of the blackness filled the field of vision of that eye. It was like I was keeping my right eye diverted, keeping it prepared for an escape route or for a reassuring glance at something I understood might protect me. Inexplicably, somehow my twisting continued anyway until I could see the entire blackened shape behind me.

It appeared to be swaying gently from side-to-side,

as if it were made of chiffon and was hanging suspended in an evening breeze. It didn't appear to be touching the floor, or at least I couldn't see any folds of it lying on it. Whatever it was or was wearing hung downward perfectly straight its entire length. I next forced myself to begin looking upwards from the floor to see the intruder's entire body, shape or size. At that point I still had no idea what was either happening or what it was that appeared behind me. It might have been Tom pulling some prank, the other patient wandering around the laboratory in a costume or me simply having some kind of sleep-deprived hallucination. I couldn't let myself panic beyond the point I already was. With all the will power I possessed, I made myself take the last step in this examination process and look fully and directly at this unknown and progressively terrifying form.

It's only months later that I am able to recount all this. The intervening time has been filled with almost unspeakable visitations and events; all of which I will try desperately to record before it becomes impossible for me to do so. Even now, to recall this moment is still so horrifying.

What immediately caught my attention when I twisted fully in my swivel chair to look straight on at the form behind me was that its shape appeared to redefine itself continuously. It would appear oblong, then cylindrical, then circular, then square. But always, it heaved to and fro, like it was having difficulty getting enough air to breathe. There were no appendages that I could identify with that first look. But when it wanted to address me, it did assume a more upright and stationary position.

It was black. So much so that it appeared to absorb any light around it. It was like a sink that sucked any ambient light into it, and I immediately had the feeling that I, too, was somehow being drawn into it. It seemed almost to have its own magnetic field, as if it were an object that was independent of any worldly mass, as if it could exist independent of what we humans call an earthly home. Almost immediately upon seeing it in its fullness, I had the awful impression that it was from far, far away. Not only did it not belong here on this world, but that its presence signaled something terribly menacing was about to happen... to me, to my patients here that night or to countless others. Nothing about its appearance, the way it first presented itself in REM stage sleep my last two all-night, uninterrupted studies or the circumstance of it standing behind me at that moment foretold anything but the most extreme danger... for everyone. I sensed it. I knew it.

The very last of the few distinguishing features it possessed were its two eyes and how they were positioned on the top of its almost shapeless mass of blackness. They were each as large as an old silver dollar that I once was given by my grandfather as a good luck charm. Neither eye had lids or lashes. There was no blinking or shifting side to side or up and down. They only stared straight ahead, unblinkingly. And they were much further apart than any human or animal of its size would normally dictate. There had to be a good four to five inches between them, and they were positioned almost at the top of its slightly more narrowed and rounded top surface; I guess you could call it at the very top of its head., but there was no actual cranium or forehead that I could recognize; nor did there appear to be any shoulders or extremities. The only visible features it seemed to possess were the eyes; a pure, suspended and weaving/heaving blackness and its stony and paralyzing silence. It simply stared at me.

Eventually, in what seemed like an endless period of time, I finally managed to force myself to exhale in a hoarse whisper. "Who are you? What are you doing here?" And then, now in retrospect, I added what had to be the most idiotic statement this invader had ever heard upon its first appearance before a total stranger, "This is a private office and laboratory."

As if it didn't already know this or care. It was just my simplistic way of trying to maintain some meager amount of reality and normalcy. I desperately needed to establish and maintain that there was still a concrete place in the here and now; a place that incorporated both my origin and my ongoing existence. Otherwise, I knew I would begin to fade into a dreamlike state of pure panic and madness.

But initially, there was no response or reply. No movement other than the rhythmical heaving to and fro was visible. No blinking. No sounds. It just stared straight at me, as if it were sizing me up for some kind of attack. That made me even more unhinged.

"Can you speak?!" I eventually managed to blurt out in a louder, almost hysterical voice. "What are you doing here? You must leave… by whatever means you came into this laboratory. We are in the midst of studies, and I do not want you to disturb the patients. Do you understand me? Speak up or leave!!"

And as I sputtered out that last demand, I began to rise from my armchair. But believe me, it was not to confront the intruder. Most likely, I was going to make a frantic dash out of the office and try to lock its two doors before it got outside the office area. Obviously, it was a stupid thought. Apparently this creature didn't use doors. That was fairly evident by this time. And honestly, this outburst took all the heroic impulses that were or ever had resided in me. I was spent. Sheer panic was my next and only option.

"Sit down!!" were the first words that I heard from the blackened form.

"And pay attention. You are going to have to halt your impulse to panic and run. For the sake of life… yours and everyone else's…, you need to listen carefully to what I have to say.

"My presence here is no curious event to be reported in the national or international media. And certainly you are going to have to stop broadcasting your witnessing the two so-called anomalies in the two sleep tests prior to this one. Succinctly put, they were me probing your lab and your reactions to them. For now, even your communication with your immediate supervisor must stop. Far too much is at stake for your entire world for it to become the subject of conjecture and debate. There simply is no time left to be spent in conjecture or idle supposition. Brace up! Listen very carefully to me! There is little time remaining. They are coming, and even at this moment the invasion is probably beginning."

Mustering up all the calm that I could at hearing this, I sank back down in my arm chair, staring straight ahead at the blob in front of me in shock and horror. Even as it spoke, there were no extra bodily movements, indicating that it even had a mouth. It was like hearing a recorded message, and it was beyond my ability to grasp the substance of what had been said thus far or to appreciate any of it. By now, I became convinced that it was I who was dreaming, and not just the study patients. I shook my head vigorously side to side to wake up. Then I rubbed my eyes and slapped the side of my face, something that was not uncommon for me to do during the night when I felt myself losing concentration and alertness. And having done this, I again refocused and looked again behind me, expecting it to be vacant of any blackened form and confirm that I had been hallucinating.

And at that point, the sheer horror of all my life's failures, imaginings and predictions came back into focus. The shapeless form was still suspended in front of me, but now it had come closer.

"How am I supposed to grasp or understand what you tell me? I mumbled. "And how do you expect me to not be afraid... even terrified at this moment? Why are you telling me these things? I am nobody. I know very few people. I'm no good at describing even the most remarkable or beautiful vista or scene. My communication skills are non-existent. Why else would anyone end up at the end of their work life sitting here in isolation, working with people who are simply sleeping? You've made a big mistake. I'm not your person to deliver anything... to anybody. Nobody would listen to me; they never have before. Why should they now?

"And if what you tell me is so urgent, why didn't you meet with the leaders of the world. Tell them. You must be new at this sort of thing. Or if somebody or something sent you here, you need to communicate back to them, that they made a major mistake. Your coordinates were off. You landed in the wrong place.

"My best and only advice right now, given the desperate urge for me to start screaming at the top of my lungs, is to back-track and begin again somewhere closer to the centers of power. An isolated sleep lab, situated in a rather remote region that is sparsely populated, isn't it. I'm too dumb and inarticulate to help you with whatever you have in mind. Besides, how am I supposed to believe anything you tell me? Please. Just leave. I won't tell anyone, not even Tom, all this has happened. That's a heartfelt promise. Please go. I beg you."

Following my rather lengthy response, there again was some uncomfortable silence. It was all the more so because the black form did not make any effort to leave or disappear.

"You are wasting my time," it curtly replied to my self-description and plea. "You underestimate me if you think that I'm not already aware of you and your strengths and weaknesses. Your hesitation and doubts are valid... to a point. But henceforth you are to do exactly what I tell you. Don't bother me with questions or excuses. In time I will tell you what you need to know for the particular assignment that I will give you. But at this point, you need none of that. Besides, there just is not the time. Your patients will be needing your attention shortly.

"So let me complete this introductory meeting by simply saying that you have been chosen for what is going to be asked of you because of how you have sequenced your dreaming and secondarily, for who you are and for what potentially you can do. If time allows in the future, I will explain in detail the meaning and significance of these qualifications.

"And I need to conclude by issuing you a communication device, along with some instructions of its function and usage; and finish up with your first orders. Be advised, before I do: you have absolutely no choice in this matter. Ignore me, these instructions or divulge what has happened here to anyone other than to whom I instruct you to tell, and you, along with all that you see about you will change completely and violently. And if my saying this to you startles and terrifies you, it is meant to.

"Once I exit here, you will find a device resting on your workbench that you are to attach to your left wrist immediately. It will look and functions like one of your normal wrist watches. And it will keep accurate time to avoid needless questions and curiosity. But it is how you and I will communicate in the next few hours. If I need to speak with you, it will vibrate. And if you need to speak to me, you simply push in the small knob on the hand side of the device. That will alert me. In either case, you are to walk briskly to somewhere less conspicuous and just speak. You do not need to hold your wrist up to you mouth. Speak in a normal voice. You need not whisper or speak loudly.

"Just the same, you may be thinking that if I can do all that has happened up until this moment with the sleep cycles and my appearance here tonight, why don't I just tap into your thoughts, like I can do yours or anyone else's dreams? I can and could. But that means that I have to be more aware of you than I have time to be. While you are doing my bidding, I will be extremely busy trying to affect changes and make other preparations. You are a cog in a vast network. And the success of our efforts will most likely not be readily known by either of us. There is so much you do not know at this time. Over time I will attempt to fill in when and where I can. It will be on a 'need to know' basis, as your military/secret service folks are fond of saying.

"Lastly, I have one last order for you tonight. After you finish this night's work, you are to notify your supervisor that you need to take the rest of this week off. Simply say it is for emergency reasons, which it most certainly is. And then I need you to get to Washington, D.C. as quickly as you can. I will give you further orders as necessary. Do you have any pertinent questions?"

"How will I know what you are telling me and asking of me is legitimate?" I managed to whisper.

"You'll see soon enough after I leave you in a few moments."

"I'm scared," I said, as my voice trailed off.

"Good. So am I. Now, do as I have commanded."

After having said that, as I was looking straight at the blacked form, it disappeared. Being overcome with fright and doubt as to my sanity and the reality of any of this, I gradually turned my swivel chair toward the computer keyboard and my patients' ongoing studies, and there positioned in the middle of the desk was what appeared to be a regular size wristwatch. The face of it was blank. Despite my forebodings and reluctance, I reached forward and expanded the interlocking, metal band and slipped it on my left wrist. I never wore a wrist watch. For years I either used a traditional pocket watch or just purchased a modest wrist watch and took the band off and carried the face in my pocket.

Immediately upon getting the wrist watch on my wrist, there appeared an exact image of the blackened form and then the face was transformed into a standard watch face with the hands indicating that is was 4:50 a.m. This entire encounter which was to forever alter my life, and everyone else's on this planet, took only twenty minutes.

WASHINGTON, D.C.

FIVE: THE NEW REALITY

Honestly, after my initial encounter with my living-nightmare visitation, I don't remember unhooking or discussing anything about their studies with my two patients prior to their leaving the clinic. I do remember that one of the patients when he was about to leave the laboratory mentioned the presence of an unusual odor in his bedroom. He said it was like ammonia. It reminded him of the intense smell he associated with his cleaning out the chicken shed when he was a boy, and how the odor always got stronger the closer it got to being done. He was describing exactly what I had smelled when I was first aware of the awful visitor's presence in the office. I tried to fend off his remark by fabricating a story about the building recently having problems with its sewer lines. But his look upon exiting the front door indicated he knew it was too intense an odor for that to be the case. And besides, he added, he had a terrific headache, which seemed to be getting worse with each passing minute. Still reeling from all I had been told and was supposed to do, I recalled suddenly that this was the same patient to whom the dark form had appeared briefly in his bedroom and that had the multiple stain-like intrusions on his computer tracing. I knew immediately his complaints were well-founded, and I could only hope there would be no lasting aftereffects for him.

My mind was frantic by the time I had cleaned up the patient's rooms, sorted out the equipment and completed the final download of the two night's studies. I felt myself slipping into emotional and mental paralysis. I had to go home. There was no way I could stay in that office another minute, once I had finished my work. Hurriedly, I scribbled a note to Tom indicating that I had to take the rest of the week off for personal business. I apologized for the suddenness of my request but indicated that it was very urgent that I do so. And violating the instructions I had just been given, I said I would fill him in on the details of my reason for this request upon my return to work the next week.

But by the time I had completed that note, the oppressiveness of the dark and deathly quiet laboratory had thoroughly unnerved me. The combination of its omnipresent isolation and stillness filled me with a dread unlike any I had ever imagined possible, short of what someone might experience just before having a near death experience. I was convinced that I had had an encounter with a messenger of death or with Death itself earlier that morning. And I sensed my privacy and safety had been sacrificed in some way. I was now a pawn on a game board that incorporated everything around me. I fled the lab for home and its relative safety. The light of dawn that greeted me as I exited the basement doorway onto the parking lot provided me some needed comfort. It was like I never wanted to be in a darkened area or sleep again.

Once home, I quickly fixed and ate some cold cereal, sprinkled with bits of canned fruit. Exhausted from just two night's work and my indescribable encounter with the alien form just a few hours ago, I stumbled into the bedroom and collapsed into fitful and almost dreamless sleep.

I say "almost", because it wasn't totally dreamless or possibly better described, totally uninterrupted. In what I can only recall as a vivid and lifelike experience, sometime during the only dream sequence I believe I had during that morning's nap, the blackened, talking shape manifested itself again. And it briefly spoke directly at me, in words that I recalled exactly, as if they were meant not to be forgotten upon my awakening.

They were: "Tell no one of my appearance today. Do what I have instructed! Your round-trip airline tickets to Washington, D.C. will be waiting for you at the WestAir ticket counter for flight number 1024, which leaves at 2:30 p.m. this afternoon for Washington, D.C. Be on it. You will have further instructions during your flight and upon your arrival. Do not worry about accommodations; they will be taken care of as well. Stay alert! You are in grave danger. The process of selection and removal has already begun. You may already be too late."

Recalling these words verbatim did nothing to ease my mind about what had been happening over the last few days. But shaking off the nervousness as much as possible, I became determined to end this rash of coincidents and apparitions, which had to be due to exhaustion, by calling the toll free number for the WestAir reservations in order to put to rest this entire matter. I knew I was becoming over wrought and that the airline representative would have no idea what I was referring to when I asked for some confirmation of a ticket in my name for a flight today to

Washington, D.C.

Thumbing through the yellow pages, I eventually located the correct number and called them. Excusing myself, being somewhat embarrassed by this entire matter, I asked about my having any flight reservation for today. There followed the usual security questions regarding my full name, address, telephone number and mother's maiden name.

After I supplied all these, the chipper voice on the other end of the line, replied "Yes, sir, Mr. Pruitt, your tickets will be waiting for you at our ticket counter. Please arrive at the airport at least two hours ahead of your scheduled departure. Have a safe trip, and thank you for choosing WestAir."

Mustering up all the reserve congeniality I could, I thanked her and dropped the telephone receiver into its cradle. At the same time, I slumped into the armchair next to the phone. From the instant I got this confirmation I knew, without any doubt, that my life was forever changed and something so awful was about to happen... or had already begun.

Then, in an act of defiance, I reached down and removed the device the "stain" had told me to wear. If it was going to invade my unconscious mind as well, what was the sense of wearing it? All I had to do was doze and I would be getting instructions and orders. And besides, it reminded me of a location bracelet, which paroled felons wore. Enough was enough... even at the very beginning of my being told what to do and to whom.

My desperate attempts to organize and however modestly adapt to the world around me was failing. It was a place I had been unable to understand or to succeed in even before the greatest tragedy of my life: the death of my family. And now it was crumbling further away by the second. I felt myself slipping into what others have described as certain insanity. Any reality I once knew was rapidly disappearing beneath and around me. And I was frightened beyond words to describe the emotion. Never mind the usual questions: "Why me?"; "What's all this actually about?"; "Who, in fact, is this sinister intruder?" or "Is this really happening to me?" There wasn't time to ask them nor was there any reason to believe the answers if they came... by whatever means. I was alone. And I had absolutely no idea who, what or why this was happening.

In desperation, I glanced over at the wall clock my wife and I bought for ourselves as our first house-warming gift, following a devastating house fire, in which we lost everything. Its steady ticking and chiming had always comforted us. But today, it seemed to be mute. All sounds around me were dampened, like that which you experience when surrounded by a thick, coastal fog. The only sounds I heard or felt were those associated with the pounding of my heart. And it was racing uncontrollably. It was as if it sensed that its host was in such danger that it wanted to flee.

The clock chimed 11:30 a.m. I had one hour to pack and get to the airport. What if I didn't do it? What if I just ignored this madness and went about my daily chores like nothing had happened? What if? What if?

And just then the telephone rang, causing me to lurch forward in my armchair. Convinced that it was probably the black messenger calling to threaten me, I cautiously picked up the phone and timidly answered, "Yes..."

"Conner, this is Tom. What's up with your needing the week off?"

Dizzy with shock and confusion, I had to pause before replying.

"Hey, are you ok?" he followed up. "What's going on? Are you sick? Do you need some kind of surgery?"

"No, no; it's nothing like that," I was finally able to force myself to reply. "But it is a grave emergency; one that I can't give you the details about yet. And that's because I don't even know myself what is happening. I just know I have been told to go immediately to Washington, D.C. Any more than that I can't say."

"Can't or won't?"

"Well, to be perfectly honest... both," I answered. "It's all so crazy, but you've got to believe me. It is a true emergency, and I have been given no choice but to leave. You can dock my pay, and I promise to never do this kind of thing again. It wouldn't be happening now, but I have been given no choice."

"Why the hush-hush? That's not like you. I usually can't shut you up."

"It's part of the instructions I have been given."

"Sounds like government-related stuff... I sure hope you're not in some kind of trouble with the feds. I know you had some tax problems a few years back. But I'll respect your need for privacy. Just try to keep me as informed as you can through this next week. Colleen and I worry about you, after your loss of Abby and Jason. In the meantime, is there anything I can do for you while you're gone?"

"Can you come over and get George. I know you'd feed him, but he really likes you two and would be less stressed if he was at your place this week. For such a protective breed of dog, he sure has transferred some of that loyalty to you folks."

"Sure thing. I'll come over after work today and get him. Set out his food and leash. I've still got your front door key, don't I?"

"I'm sure you do. If not, look for one taped underneath the newspaper container. And if you will, please pick up the newspapers and my mail any time you can think of it. I'm not going to have time to stop either. I've got to get out of here and be at the airport by 12:30 p.m."

"Mercy, you haven't been given much time. So, I won't keep you any longer. Take care of yourself, friend. We'll be thinking about you, and don't worry about the lab. I'll get Kay to come in for you the rest of this week. She needs the extra hours anyway. And remember: keep in touch. And have a safe trip."

"Thanks for being so understanding. I'll keep you updated… as much as I can."

From that moment on until I arrived at the airport is a period of time that has vanished from my memory. The combination of fear, anxiety and anticipation had by then so ravaged my ability to organize and remember that I simply began doing things by rote: get out an old canvas travel bag, one which could easily be taken on board and stowed in the luggage bin overhead, pack a few toiletries without attempting to clean up or shave, set out some clean water and refill George's food pan with dog food, check my wallet for my one and only credit card, get the truck keys and lock the front and back doors.

The airport was about ten miles from my apartment. I had been there a couple of times either to pick up a family member or a close friend, but I had never flown out of there myself. In fact, I had only flown a few times before this; all of them associated with my being in the Army and going back and forth to stateside duty stations or for overseas deployment. I had no romantic visions about flying. The military flights were not ones that I ever wanted to recall, given the nature of my assignments and their outcomes. I saw combat and more importantly I saw the ravages of it over and over. Fear and dread are not new emotions for me; they are just ones I have tried to escape. But this command I have been given and the circumstances surrounding it have brought all those times back to me. If anything, it only added to my feelings of fear and the incomprehensible ability to understand why I had been picked to make this trip to Washington, D.C. of all places; and for it to be by a shadowy being of such unknown and probably unknowable origins.

After I parked in the long term parking area for flight departures, I walked to the airport entrance and began a numbing process of venturing into the absolute unknown. Would the ticket agent have any idea what I was asking? Would I even have tickets, as I had been assured I would have in my silly dream?

Again, to my shock and amazement, when it came my turn to approach the prepaid ticket counter and inquire as to whether there had been a round-trip ticket reserved for me to Washington, D.C., after a brief exchange regarding my personal information, I was informed that indeed there was. And furthermore, that it was not in the "Coach" section but was in "Business Class".

Then once the agent asked about my luggage, double-checked by driver's license for confirmation of my identity, I was given the tickets, a boarding pass and wished a safe and pleasant holiday. It took all the self-control that I could muster up at the moment, to refrain from shouting out that this was no holiday nor was it a trip I planned, arranged or even had the vaguest idea why I was taking. But instead, I tried to smile weakly and thanked him, after asking which way was the concourse and gate I was supposed to use.

From that point on until it was announced in the waiting area that it was time for all Business Class ticket holders to come forward to enter the waiting plane, I just kind of moved along with the crowd of people, allowing them to herd me in the direction I was supposed to go. There is absolutely no definition of time or place for this entire period. My fear and confusion were becoming unbearable. Twice I had to find a restroom before the call to board the plane and vomited, along with having uncontrollable diarrhea. Even if the rest of me was unsure what to do in the present circumstances, my stomach and bowels sure knew. They fled.

Upon entering the ramp which was to take us into the immense plane, I looked around and saw that all my fellow travelers were stylishly dressed and seemed fully prepared and motivated for their trip ahead. Little did they know that traveling in their midst was someone who had not the slightest idea why or where he was going, once he exited this plane in a few hours. All I knew at that point was that its destination was Washington, D.C. and that my seat number was 3 B in the Business Class section.

It didn't take me long to shuffle down the aisle and see my designated seat; it was not the window seat, which was a relief to me. The aisle seat would allow me easy access to the nearby restroom, which I was certain by that time I would be using frequently. But to my disappointment, once I made my way to the seat and stowed my ragged canvas carry-on bag into the overhead compartment, already seated beside me was a very well dressed woman, who appeared to be approximately my same age… the early 50's.

Seeing her dressed like a well groomed professional seemed to drain the last of whatever coping reserve I had left in me. Folks like her intimidated me; all thoughts and self-expression became garbled. I had little formal education beyond high school, and so did my wife of twenty-three years. But both of us loved to read and were avid followers of local, national and international news. Neither of us was comfortable in formal settings or around accomplished individuals with weighty educational credentials. I became mute in their presence. So much of my conversation in a public arena, whether it was with the patients I worked with, or in any social setting, involved my life's experiences and were always antidotal. Weighty conversations left me speechless. I usually understand a lot of what was being discussed, but I was categorically unable to participate in them. I was both intimidated and my contributions were muddled and nonsensical. And due to my limited exposure, to have any such conversation alone with this professional-looking woman was doubly intimidating. I could only hope I would sleep all the way and avoid any conversation.

After pulling down a small pillow and closing the overhead bin, I briefly looked over at the person who was sitting next to me and tried to manage a relatively non-inviting nod and greeted her with an uninviting, "Good afternoon." Saying that I hoped would signal that I acknowledged her presence, but didn't encourage any more conversation. Quickly, I positioned the pillow behind my head, fumbled at adjusting the foot and back rest and closed my eyes. I sincerely hoped that I could immediately fall asleep, along with offering a silent, solitary prayer to all that was holy and Ever-Present, that the darkened form would not invade my dream state, should I drift into one.

But to my added horror, if that was possible after all that had been happening since 4:30 that morning, the person next to me spoke up, as I closed my eyes and offered up my prayer. "No, that won't be happening Conner; mainly, because I am now sitting next to you."

My eyes popped open with such suddenness and force I'm sure it was audible throughout the cabin. And just as quickly I whipped my head around and looked squarely into the deepest blue eyes I'd ever seen anywhere. Before me was the most elegantly dressed and coiffured individual I had ever seen. There was no comparison to what I had been exposed to in the sleep lab earlier this same day. And there was the permeating fragrance of lavender that enveloped me as I stared at the person or thing next to me; it wasn't the strong ammonia odor that earlier had permeated the sleep lab.

"YOU!!" I shouted, to the surprise and shock of passengers already seated or in the process of doing so.

"Lower your voice!" the person beside me commanded. "This is neither the time nor the place to bring attention to you or to me. Now I want you to say, in not so loud a voice, "What a wonderful surprise! How long has it been since we last saw each other?"

Summing up courage to speak from somewhere in an unknown region of my psyche, I did as I was instructed. But if anyone was really watching all this unfold, it would have been very clear to them that rather than delight and wonder, my look and body language indicated the complete opposite of "wonderful". I wanted with all my heart and soul to start screaming in anguish and horror and never stop.

"Calm down, Connor!" she demanded. "I'm not here to harm, frighten or taunt you, even though you've only just seen me as I probed and then spoke with you in the lab earlier this morning. And I'm not forgetting the chilling news I initially gave you about the winnowing process that was beginning as we initially spoke or about the nonnegotiable order for you to board this flight to Washington, D.C. or why you of all people were chosen to help slow or halt the process that is now underway.

"Right now I want you to turn around and raise your hand and request of the soon-to-be passing cabin attendant that you'd like two glasses of champagne for us to celebrate a surprising reunion of old classmates. She will be starting to walk this way about now. Do it! Be pleasant and genuinely surprised as you make the request. As of right now your mission, which is far more important than you could ever image, has begun. Buck up, buster. The curtain is rising, and this is no dress rehearsal."

Something then happened to me. It was almost as if all the cells in my body and the filaments of my soul came together and acknowledged that this was my do or die moment. But unlike what I had experienced in combat, where I was always surrounded by my brothers-in-arms, I knew I was alone now. If anything had prepared me for this, I sure was unaware of it. As I turned to call out to the approaching stewardess, a brief prayer crossed my lips: "Holy God, be with us all…"   And I smiled and ordered the two drinks.

SIX: MY ASSIGNMENT BEGINS

The non-stop flight from the west coast to Washington, D.C. took over five hours as calculated by anyone else's normal measurement of time.   And yet there is another method to record time's passage; one that is etched in or throughout your psyche and soul. Unquestionably, if the telling of this story serves no other purpose, let me assure you at this early stage there is such an entity as the soul.   That fact was made clear in the most absolute of terms during the next three weeks.   I found that there are events and times that seem to cause time, itself, to even stand still.   But your soul is always monitoring time's progress or the advent of it being hijacked, and mine began that process in earnest after our two drinks arrived.

Never one to know exactly how or even what to drink in a social setting, which this encounter was anything but, I gulped down the contents of the glass brought to us without knowing or caring what it was.   Then wiping my mouth after inhaling it, I turned in my cushioned, oversized seat and faced the strikingly beautiful but terrifyingly awful being sitting beside me and addressed it with all the forthrightness I could muster.

"Ok," I began, having lowered my voice just above a

whisper, "Now that you've given me this opportunity to face you again, but this time in a less isolated setting and with your appearance somewhat less daunting, I need some reassurance from you or at least some idea of what you are planning on doing that will possibly keep me from leaping up from this seat and run screaming down the aisle to the flight crew's cabin.

"It is probably obvious to you by now that I am at the very bottom of anyone's list of candidates for any assignment or mission, much less for dealing with some morphing extraterrestrial. I am invisible to anyone outside that night lab you seemed to find so intriguing and invaded without any permission or invitation. But my social invisibility serves at least one purpose: it allows me to adjust to and to cope with unexpected or unrehearsed situations at my own pace.

"That said; you aren't allowing me that possibility. You are pushing me pell-mell into what I can only describe as an imminent, full-dress enactment of hell on earth. And I need to know why. Why me? Who are you? Where do you come from? What is all this doom and gloom about? Is there some process now underway that is uncontrollable and inevitable or can it be delayed or avoided? And, most importantly, what has happened locally or worldwide that caused you to come to our laboratory, of all the options available to you, in the first place?

"I need some answers. Whatever you think or know about me, by now you also must be aware that I am not very intelligent. You have to be more forthright. I sense I have no choice about whether I help you, but you're not going to have much luck with me if you don't give me some details. I will simply become uncontrollably hysterical. Believe me. My psyche is on the very edge of that precipice at this moment. It would take very little for me to slip into a mute state. Talk to me!… please…"

My plea was followed by a period of silence that in itself added to my nervousness and sense of impending panic. Throughout this period, the strange apparition never changed her expression or made any bodily movements. It was like she went into some kind of trance state. She just looked straight ahead. Finally, she reached forward and took the glass of champagne and drank it slowly, placed it back on her backrest tray, then turned slowly and looked me squarely in the eyes. It was a look of absolute, unemotional, concentration. There was no warmth, no smile, nothing to reassure me that what I was about to hear was going to comfort me. And then she spoke.

"Let me be frank. It is not in my nature to be generous of spirit or freely discuss what the possibilities are or likelihoods for the upcoming future of a civilization that I and my associates are in the beginning stages of consuming. Neither do I feel especially motivated to spell out to you what is to be your role, however minor, in the following days. For one thing, I am not sure what the outcome of our meeting will be tomorrow. Much depends on our reception and the willingness and openness of your President. If she is not prepared to accept what I tell her, your role will only be that of a lab rat.

"As you, yourself, have so frequently admitted, in describing your shortcomings, I, too, do not honestly think you have the fortitude or intelligence to be of much more help to me than that of a demonstration manikin. Already, you have tried my patience more than I usually will tolerate."

"Then why did you force me into coming with you?" I hissed, now realizing her disdain and low opinion of me.

54

"Because it was quick and easy. You were alone. You were too afraid to put up a fight or much of a protest. In practically every other similar situation elsewhere, like when you and I first met, I usually have to forage over a number of weeks to find someone as docile and intimidated as you were. Not to deflate you even further, but you leave me completely unimpressed. I doubt there is a brave or daring cell circulating throughout your body at this moment. But saying that, you will be perfect for the objective I have to meet tomorrow.

"So, try and find some measure of composure. And try to accept that you are not going to know ahead of time what my appearance in your sleep laboratory indicates or what the purpose of my wanting to speak with the person who holds the highest office in your land involves. You will know what you need to as the circumstances dictate.

"For now, you need to get some rest. You have been up all last night and have not had a chance to sleep any today. I need you more refreshed and alert tomorrow. If you are exhausted, on top of being a weak and rather pitiful excuse for a citizen soldier, the danger ahead for your country and world increases exponentially.

"To conclude, you only need to know that you and I will be traveling together for the remainder of this trip. And that includes our staying together tonight. I do not want to lose sight of you; it will be too awkward getting a replacement at this late date. Think of yourself, if you like, as my prisoner. Only time will tell if your role expands beyond that. I will brief you on what happens next once this flight concludes. This is all you need to know for now."

From the conclusion of this rebuke to my awaking the next morning in our hotel room, situated a few blocks from the White House, I said very little and only then because of witnessing the greatest shock and horror imaginable.

I finished my drink in silence and positioned my armchair in a reclined position and closed my eyes. The next thing I remember hearing was when the airplane's pilot announced that we were about to begin our final approach to the Dulles International Airport. But there was one small difference in my silence now. Rather than being intimidated and cowered, I was starting to become angry. For me, anger has always been the refreshment of choice when I slowly crawl out from under my shroud of intimidation and reticence. This was one "lab rat" that was not going to be herded into some execution chamber blindly or docilely.

Once the passengers in the Business Class were given the ok to exit the airplane, I stood back and allowed my extraterrestrial jailer to proceed out ahead of me. No words or glances were exchanged. It was as if she had uttered an unspoken command: "Keep Silent and Follow Me".

And it being late afternoon, the terminal was seething with surging currents of travelers, and their families, friends or associates doggedly weaving and bumping their way along with them. I closely followed my guide, as she occasionally, even in the densest crowd, was looking around to make sure I was not lost or had wandered off.

My chance of escape from this madness came when I spied someone entering a doorway which was marked, "Authorized Personnel Only". In an instant, I diverted from closely following my captor and ducked in behind the individual who had opened the secured door.

As I did so, I excused myself and urgently whispered to him, "I am being kidnapped and need your protection. I need you to take me immediately to someone in airport security. Please… please help me."

As I heard the security door snap shut behind me, I turned quickly to see if the transformed stain had been able to follow me. Luckily, there was no one. My escape, so far, had been successful. Or so I thought.

In the dim light of the hallway the airport employee replied, "I'm not a security officer, but I will call someone who can provide you the assistance you apparently need."

No sooner had he cleared his throat to speak into his headset, when to my absolute surprise the woman-appearing-alien sitting next to me throughout the just-concluded flight appeared behind him, facing me, and clasped both her hands around the airport employee's head. In an instant he fell to the ground… lifeless.

Rebuking me, she off-handedly said, in the most unnerving, casual voice, "That senseless death was your doing."

Shocked, I lunged backward, exclaiming, "You killed that innocent man!"

"On the contrary," she answered, "You did. I warned you. Let this be a lesson. Do not attempt anything or do anything that I haven't previously instructed you to do… you silly earthling! Now open that door and let us proceed out the terminal and find a taxi cab. We need to get to our hotel as soon as possible. I have a lot to do before tomorrow's meeting."

And that was it. There was no expression of remorse. No acknowledgement of her taking a life. It was as if she had just casually bumped into someone in a crowded hallway. Taking a life warranted no comment. It seemed perfectly natural. And the ease with which she performed the killing was gruesome and terrifying. I instantly thought of my patients in the sleep laboratory and of what this invasion must mean for all humanity. The impact of what I was experiencing was finally taking a firm hold at my core. I was on the very front line of this world's possible annihilation.

SEVEN: THE WHITE HOUSE

My memory of what happened next is vague. But the one that wasn't was my recalling the murder of the airport security employee. Whatever doubts I had about my safety or about the eventual purpose and goal of this invader of our sleep laboratory had vanished. The beginnings of any conflict or war be it local, national or worldwide, must often be buried in what seemed rather inconsequential decisions or actions. It must often take generations for historians to ferret out the twisted logic and deterioration leading up to the first shot fired or bomb dropped. It will not be so with this conflict that I am witnessing in its infancy. If I should live long enough to fully record the events and characters involved, the progression will scream for anyone's attention and need for preparation and for a defense. No mighty army is going to stop this invasion. Of that I was certain, even at that early stage of it. I only hoped that I could discover the cause of their appearance and what might thwart their completely overpowering us as a world.

I do remember climbing into a taxi and being driven to a large hotel with an ornate lobby. And I recall that the desk clerk appeared a little puzzled that my captor approached the Reception Desk instead of me. It seemed he watched me rather intently as I hung back, while the exchange of personal information and a financial payment was arranged. I further remember him saying that the weather here in Washington, D.C. would be considerably cooler than what we had been experiencing in Palm Springs, and that he hoped we would enjoy our stay at the hotel.

Once we got to our hotel room, I was asked whether I needed anything to eat. To which I only shook my head and immediately lay down on the large sofa in an overly spacious room, whose actual purpose could only be guessed. For a brief stay, which the majority of any reservations had to be for an accommodation like this, I was sure it was far too expensive to serve as a residence for long-term use, it was too decorative and impersonal. Adding to the rather forlorn nature of the room, there was a faux fireplace. It actually served to make the room seem colder. But the sofa was conspicuously huge and overstuffed, and it seemed to envelope me as I collapsed into its interior. If my captor had any final instructions for me at that point, I was not conscious enough for any of them to register. I literally fell into one of my choreographed dreamtime sleeps. But more on that later.

Apparently, my vile roommate, if I could be so flippant using that connection, spent the night in a separate bedroom. Unbeknownst to me, she somehow rigged our hotel room's door into the hallway so that I could not have escaped, even if I wanted to try. And our being on the fifteenth floor assured that I would not attempt a window escape, unless it was simply to end my life. But, again, that avenue of escape was blocked; the windows were all permanently sealed. The air we breathed and the atmosphere we rented was all self-contained and artificial.

This atmosphere served as my introduction to Washington, D.C. and all that takes place within it.   But all that was soon to be changed… forever.

I was awakened the next morning around 7 a.m. with a jab to my shoulder and a cursory, "Wake up.   You need to get ready and have something to eat before we walk over to the White House."

Surprisingly, when my escort checked us in the evening before, she had ordered a breakfast for me to be delivered at this time.   However, if she ate anything, I never knew.   I never saw her eat, and I had no desire to ask her what she did, if she did.   Somehow, I had the impression, given my initial experience in the sleep laboratory, that any nourishment beings like her would partake of would be either offensive or gruesomely terrifying.   And feeling like I did about her, or it, I didn't really care if she poisoned my food in some manner.   My life at that moment seemed destined to end soon; that was becoming all too apparent.   And if it happened while eating what at least looked appetizing, that seemed as good an alternative as I might have in the hours or days left to me.

So I quickly washed and shaved with the sundry items for me she had also arranged to have delivered that morning and then sat down at an oversized dining table and ate alone.   While doing so, she began to brief me on what to expect would happen that morning, once we left the hotel room.   And it was while I ate that I took the time to look over at her, as she sat across from me.

Her appearance was truly remarkable.   Whoever was her makeup artist and wardrobe manager did a fine job.   But it is equally stunning how someone could be so handsomely groomed, coiffed and dressed, but without an accompanying smile or projecting an indwelling sense of

61

good will, her overall appearance was forlorn. Her eyes, if you reached past their obvious beauty, looked actually dead and lifeless. It was disturbingly haunting to look at her or it.

"Briefly, I want to outline what is to take place once we leave here," she began.

But on an impulse that surprised even me, I shouted back at her, "What if I refuse? What if I run out of this room once you open the door, screaming there is a killer in our midst and shout, 'RUN! EVERYONE RUN AS FAST AS YOU CAN!!' You are going to kill me in the next day or so anyway; just like you so casually murdered that airport employee. Refusing now to go any further will just hasten the inevitable…"

"You underestimate the skills I possess for accomplishing the tasks ahead." she interrupted me. "Taking a life, as you witnessed yesterday, is only one of many that I have, and it is one of the least demanding or impressive. For instance, you are now beginning to experience a minor, but distinct discomfort, inching its way from the base of your neck, working its way up into your occiput. Soon it will spread across and up the full extent of your cranium. There will not be any lasting damage, but as it envelopes you, you will experience various symptoms, as you are beginning to notice even now: dimness of vision, ringing in your ears with my voice becoming more distant, numbness in all your limbs, and an ache that is beginning about now to course throughout your torso and also spreading out to your four extremities. Shall I let it continue? Or are you ready to listen to what I have to say?"

Despite my longing to end my involvement in this ever-expanding day and night horror, I whimpered "Stop. I give up. Please… "

And as soon as I begged for her to have mercy on me, the symptoms ceased. Her gaze was unblinking and uncaring. It was as if what she had just administered was no more than offering someone a helping hand or putting a fine point on an argument. Nowhere in her manner or gaze was there a hint of sympathy.

"So then," she resumed, "Where were we? Oh yes, I was about to tell you we are going to walk over to the White House grounds from here. There is no need to hire a taxi or take another form of public transit. Walking will do us both good. Besides our appointment with your President is not until 9:30."

"You made an appointment with the Office of the President of the United States?!!" I exclaimed.

"Not exactly," she answered. "I simply paid her office a visit earlier this morning."

"You left me alone in here, and I knew nothing about it!"

"No, at least not in the sense that you mean 'leave'. You see, I, unlike the others of my race can move freely in both the night and daytime, noticed or invisible, whether incorporated within your dreams at night or circulating about or through you during the day. It provides me the ability to size up a situation, like I did in your sleep lab or to plan the time of an upcoming meeting like we will have later this morning with your President.

"I was able to determine through my indirect contact with her earlier this morning when she would be alone and how to make our way to her closely guarded office, without being stopped or hardly noticed. But I digress. The main thing for you to know is that we do have a time to be there, and we need to be on our way.

"Your role in this will become evident when we

finally are inside her office, and I begin to explain why I have come. And just one cautionary note. Do not attempt to alert anyone along the way where we are going. It will be useless to try. You will immediately become mute, paralyzed or worse if you speak without my permission.

"So, that said; let us be on our way. This is going to be a full day, and you have had a good night's rest."

We exited the hotel through a side door opening onto 25th Street and headed north up to K Street where the morning traffic was still quite heavy. The urge to sprint away from my imprisoned state returned; but sensing this, Finality casually reminded me, "Don't let your Earthly instincts threaten your very existence. You bolt and you die. You stay and there might be the slightest chance of hope arise out of this rapidly deteriorating threat to your planet's human inhabitants. Look straight ahead. Quit twisting your head side-to-side, as if you are about to attempt an escape. There is none: for you or anyone else at this moment. Channel your thoughts toward something more positive, and dampen down your anger. Remember: I know both your thoughts and your emotions. It's as if you're not just my physical prisoner, but my subconscious one as well. The only hope you have now is to obey my every word and channel all your strength and will into preserving what little life may soon remain on this world."

Hearing this, I sighed with growing anguish at what lay ahead and briefly nodded my head. Speaking was useless. And if she knew my thoughts… it was redundant as well. Soon we crossed 24th Street and entered the frantic swirl of traffic and pedestrians within Washington Circle. It was at that point, for the first time that I could recall, my all-knowing captor made physical contact with me by slipping her right arm around my left one and nudging me along the direction we needed to go. With her on the traffic side of the sidewalk, I knew I was boxed in and essentially immobilized. And within a few minutes afterward, we were heading southeast on Pennsylvania Avenue, while she maintained her hold of my arm the rest of the way to the White House.

Even with a heavy shirt and sweater separating my arm from hers, I could feel a distinct chill radiating from her touch. By the time we reached the Visitor's Entrance to the White House, I was almost beginning to shiver from the icy cold of her physical contact.

We walked silently block after block until we were about to cross 18th Street. Just before we stepped off the curb when the pedestrian walk-light indicated it was safe to do so, she spoke again.

"You are about to experience a strange sensation, possibly something akin to what others of your race call an 'out of body experience'. As the traffic is coming to either a stop or beginning to move and others around us are shifting to move swiftly across the street, you will suddenly become transparent, as will I. I need us to remain this way to and through most of our way into the White House and into the President's Oval Office. However, you will be able to see others around you. But undoubtedly most disturbing of all to you at the moment of transition to this state, you will also be able to see others of my kind as well. Do not panic, because of course it will be useless to scream or run. You will be invisible and voiceless to others around you. So, take a deep breath and …."

And suddenly I experienced an electrical jolt, like I had made contact with an ungrounded electrical appliance, and then I experienced what was now becoming a litany of almost nonstop terrors. If she had not been holding onto me, and essentially dragging me along, I would have become immediately paralyzed by the grotesquely bizarre sights around me. To my absolute horror, while my escort's appearance remained as it was prior to my change from being visible, as did my ability to see all the other people around me, without their being able to see me, I was now able to see countless numbers of the solid blackened objects, like the one that I saw the night before in our sleep lab office, when this alien, clutching onto me, first appeared. And adding to my horror of seeing these mostly featureless, black creatures that were presently invisible to the public was that every one of them had suddenly jerked their bodies around and were staring directly at me!

Ducking my head in shock and as a vain attempt to seem hidden from their view, I mumbled to my keeper, still holding onto my arm, "They are all looking straight at me!!"

"Yes, that's true," my captor replied. "Before this particular planetary invasion, they have never seen me convert someone to your present state. It's a first… for them and for me."

"Am I supposed to feel proud?"

"Of course not. But you might sense that my mission with you today and in the ones to follow is particularly unique. But I must add a word of caution. You having seen them in this manner, and your being with me in my transformed state has heightened their awareness of you and likely their innate aggressiveness as well."

"I cannot imagine anything being more aggressive than what I've seen with your actions since we met."

"Oh, my sleep laboratory companion, you must not become complacent or smug about what you have seen thus far. Our powers and abilities are far more lethal and destructive than anything you or anyone else on this world could have imagined. That's the reason for my having to hurry up our meeting with your President. Now, you need to focus on what is our primary objective for today: the meeting at 9:30 in the Oval Office. Worrying about future events beyond this upcoming meeting is fruitless. But it is enough to see with all my associates already here, just milling about waiting for the ok to proceed with their natural desires and abilities; we have no time to waste in worry and pointless discussions. Now, watch the curb. You will still stumble and fall if you are not careful. Just because you are invisible to your race, does not mean you can ignore the real obstacles around you. Step lively and be quiet. Your voice now carries far beyond our conversation."

Unsettled, with my deepest fears mounting by the second, I tried to regain some composure and focus on avoiding looking up and around, letting my alien invader maneuver me through the people and creatures that surged around us. And in case you are wondering, it is no thrill being invisible; at least not under these circumstances. By then, I had to try and control the constant urge to vomit from my heightening nervousness.

Soon enough we were walking past the Executive Offices and crossed West Executive Avenue. (*See Appendix: White House Complex*) And then to my surprise we were crossing onto the eighteen acre expanse of lawn, gardens and buildings of the White House. Almost dragging me by this time, I was maneuvered to the Northeast Appointment Gate, where we fell in line with a prior-approval group of sightseers. I had previously heard something about how anyone now wanting to tour the White House and its grounds had to seek clearance and confirmation from their Congressional representative. I read it took up to six months to get that approval. My own personal, alien guide positioned us at the rear of the next sight-seeing group to enter the grounds. From there we walked entirely invisible down to the Visitors' Entrance which was located between the Vermeil Room and the Library. Upon entering there our group began the actual tour, while my escort began her search for how we would enter into the White House's Central Hallway on the Ground Floor.

Hanging back further and further, as we got inside the White House, Finality, as I decided at that point to call her from then on, given the desperate circumstances that increasingly surrounded me, whispered, "We need to make our way down this long corridor until we come to the Palm Room. It separates the White House from the West Wing. (S*ee Appendix: White House West Wing Floor Plan*) Once we are inside there we may have to wait until someone exits its outside doorway into the Rose Garden area. Just the same, if no one comes soon, I have another idea how we can exit that room without being noticed. There is a guard house adjacent to the outside door, and we need to be careful about how we leave the room. We must follow closely behind the person or persons immediately ahead of us when we pass through that door leading to the West Colonnade, if that becomes possible.

"Hurry, we only have five minutes before we need to be passing through the doorway into the Oval Office. Quit hanging back. I'm almost dragging you!"

In the maze of events surrounding this particular morning's revelations and shocks, I have scant recall of what we saw once we entered the White House Grounds and Building. What I do recall with great clarity, however, was how totally surprised I was when we slipped, obviously unnoticed, into the Palm Room. Its décor and atmosphere was like breathing pure oxygen and entering a space of grace and impending promise. The color of its walls and window frames were either pure white or muted enough to accent the whiteness, and all of this served to elevate anyone's mood who entered the room. Its three walls that extended outward toward the Rose Garden and West Colonnade consisted entirely of framed glass, punctuated by various large potted plants, whose various shades of dark green blended into the lighter green wallpaper along the sides of the room's interior. (*See Appendix: White House Palm Room*).

Glancing to one side, I spied a long padded bench seat, which was located under a large painting of Lady Liberty. Having escaped from the guide and group of touring visitors, I begged my captor to please let me sit down a moment and catch my breath, and allow me the time to try and adjust, even slightly, to all that was happening to and around me. Remarkably, she agreed that I could, but only for a minute.

It was a blessed moment. I was free from being held by her icy grip and could just close my eyes and take some deep breaths. I knew I had to redouble my prior conviction to combat this invasion and my alien predator. And now I was going to soon be in the presence of the President of the United States. It was during this moment that I had to listen carefully to what was said from here on, forgetting nothing, focus on when and how to help and try to grasp why me, of all people, has been selected to accompany this awful being into this meeting. This done, I opened my eyes and nodded that I was ready to proceed.

Without any comment, Finality took my arm again and quickly opened the door that led into the Rose Garden. By doing so, it made it appear like a gust of wind blew it open. The guard sitting in the small house just outside the room rose immediately and motioned to his associate to go out to see what had caused it to swing open so violently. As we passed through it and turned right to follow the West Colonnade around to the Oval Office, I heard his companion say, "must have been a gust of wind. There is no one inside." The other guard just shrugged and mumbled something about the latch on the door needing to be checked again.

Quickly, we walked around the interior perimeter of the Rose Garden until we were just outside the door that opened into the Oval Office. Unbeknownst to me, when my captor made her uncanny visit earlier that morning to the Oval Office to check on the President's schedule, she unlocked this door and jammed it so that it would remain unlocked until our arrival.

Looking over at me, her eyes appearing as unfeeling as ever, she confounded me by saying simply, "Now begins the most impossibly difficult assignment I have ever attempted. Pay attention, Connor Pruitt! All human life that remains on this planet depends on what is said and agreed upon in this next hour."

And just as soon as she said those stunning words, she opened the Oval Office doorway, performed whatever exercise was necessary to allow us to regain our visible appearance, and announced to the Leader of the Free World, "Please excuse us Madam President, but my companion and I must borrow an hour of your time in strictest privacy, with the utmost urgent request and desperate reason for it that you will ever hear. Do not attempt to contact anyone outside this room. I have disabled all electronic equipment in this room, including all visual and recording devices. We are not here to harm you in any way."

And her next sentence really stunned me. "Indeed, we are here to try and help you preserve some human life on this world."

Spinning around and looking up from her desk, her appearance both shocked and yet remarkably curious, rather than terrified as mine would have been under the same circumstances, she replied, "Then come in. You must already know that my daily schedule is free for the next hour."

And to this, my captor, releasing my arm, answered, "Yes, I do."

EIGHT: MEETING WITH THE PRESIDENT

"Would you both like to take a seat before you get started?" the President then asked.

"Yes," my escort answered, "that would be nice. We'll both just sit on one of your sofas."

"That's fine." President Franklin replied. "And then, if you don't mind, I will also come over and sit in one of the arm chairs. I would like to position it directly in front of you; again, if you do not mind. I would rather look both of you straight on as you brief me as to what has brought you here. Obviously, I am already impressed with your abilities. No one could achieve the stealth to get into this Office undetected unless she or he had some awesome powers. You now have my undivided attention, and as you probably already know, I give strict instructions not to have any interruptions when I have the opportunity to set aside this hour-long period of work and reflection.

"And if you will, would you grant me the courtesy of knowing your names? I believe you know mine. And where do you come from? … Please."

After the President's suggestion and questions; and as she was standing up from behind her desk, covered with odd piles of papers and manila folders, and began to maneuver to a striped green and cream colored armchair, both Finality and I crossed the room and angled toward the closest white, overstuffed sofa in the middle of the room. As I nervously glanced around it, I noted the various pictures and displays, but the most striking feature of the room, aside from its oval shape, was its magnificent, light blue carpet, emblazoned with The Presidential Seal. It along with the sparing collection of pictures and other decorative and symbolic objects in the room, gave it an atmosphere of steely purposefulness. In here decisions had to be made. Conclusions had to be arrived at. Actions had to be taken. It became clear to me at that moment why my strange and terrifying nighttime intruder chose this place and person. If actions had to be taken, they would begin here.

Once the three of us were seated, the most remarkable and soul-searching conversation anyone in the history of this planet could have imagined began.

"To answer your initial question, Conner Pruitt, seated here beside me, was working in a sleep laboratory in southern California up until last night. My first appearance in his lab began a week or so before that however. In other words, to prepare for our meeting here this morning, I had to select the right place and person to begin trying to minimize what will soon become apparent to you that will be the most far-reaching, tragic and disruptive event of all time. Why exactly Conner, here, was chosen and has literally been drug here will be made clear later in this conversation. Even he is unaware as to why. And to fully answer your question, he recently began calling me 'Finality', which probably is as good a name as any for me. I have never really had need for one before this appearance on your world.

"I hail from anywhere there is trouble throughout the Universe. My stock and trade for eons has been to be the vanguard of death. I initiate the tactical plan for the end of most life on a world. And I have done so with great relish and efficiency. But in my exploratory ventures into the dreams of various ones of your species, I became more and more stunned by the remnants of something different about you, as a species. And again that brings me back to Conne. But again, any explanation of what that is will have to wait."

"Excuse me for interrupting so early in your discourse," the President interjected, "But is your usual method of appearing to others through their dreams? And is one's dreaming the pathway to whatever harm may eventually come to them?"

"Yes to both questions," came the startling reply. "It is our primary route of entry and for snatching away life."

"Then pardon me again, if you will," pressed the President, whose name was Dena Franklin, and who I understood came from the State of Maine, "what is the reason or justification you have for taking life, as you so gracefully disguise your gruesome, primary objective?"

Being a rather modest follower of current events, I did remember that President Franklin was voted into Office by a landslide three years ago, and she was the first President to be elected as an Independent. And interestingly, she has maintained a studied distance and a persistent objectivity toward the other two major political parties. Aside from the political bosses of these parties, she remains extremely popular throughout the nation and world. Hers was already a healing presidency.

"The answer to that question is simple and straightforward: because we are cosmic vultures. It is what we do. We are the cleaners of the cosmos. We scour the worlds that have lost their purpose and their way and are becoming self-destructive. We are commissioned not to allow a world to become uninhabitable. And yours is on the verge of becoming that way.

"But, as Conner here has seen, I have special powers and abilities not available to others of my kind. They were given to me for the purpose of organizing and assembling the proper number and varieties of my cohorts to as efficiently and quickly as possible fulfill our mission."

"And, on average," the President interrupted again; this time her voice had the tone of building disgust and impatience, "how long does it usually take to complete one of these 'missions', as you call them?"

"It could be anywhere from a week to several months, depending on how vast and widely distributed the particular world's population is and how many of my fellow-associates accompany me. Also, I might add that once the process has begun on an individual level, it is swift and I would add, with some pride, rather painless. Would you like me to go into detail on our methodology?"

"No, at this point that will not be necessary," snapped the President. "I'm getting the picture little by little, and none of it is pleasant or really comprehensible. How do you expect me to believe all this, despite your rather dramatic entrance and outlandish objective? Surely, the places you have been to offer overwhelming resistance, as I am sure ours would or will do. No civilization, however crude or decaying, would simply allow you to take over without an unimaginable battle for survival."

"Oh, yes, that's true; many do. But you must realize that our invasion is selective and indefensible. We enter through the portal of your dreaming, which is something that everyone does... eventually. Even if someone tries to maintain a prolonged awake state, eventually they will drop into prolonged, recovery REM sleep. And when they do, one of us is waiting patiently to consume them.

"It's like the air going out of a balloon. We tease out the reluctant spirit or soul, as you might describe it, and then ingest it and proceed to inhale the vital organs from the head downward until we have consumed the entire body. There is nothing remaining, and because we begin with the higher learning centers, there is only the briefest discomfort, which is most often only registered in the unconscious mind. Essentially, the individual is never aware of their final moments of life. And there is no trace of them left afterwards.

"Resistance is useless once we have begun our cleaning process. But as I have alluded to, this world is different. I sensed it right away when I began my planetary survey and probed Connor here and his development of a particular ability."

"Can you be more specific?" the President demanded.

"And I'd certainly be grateful if you would enlighten me as to what you are talking about," I chimed in for the first time in this all-important meeting. The words just blurted out of my mouth. I didn't think ahead or plan it. It was spontaneous and surprised even my captor.

"'Yes', for you madam President, but 'no', for you Connor. In due time I will brief Conner on what I have discovered and will want him to do, but for now my focus is on you," the foreign invader said, as she turned more directly to face the President.

"And if you will, I plan on now taking you into my confidence, while I leave Connor here to rest a bit. But be advised, Connor, you are not to move from where you are sitting. I will be monitoring your movements all the while I am speaking with the President. Do not move!"

"Madam President: do not be overly alarmed, but you will now become invisible to those around you. And in this way I can discuss very sensitive issues with you, without divulging them to Connor, here. His time to know will come later. So, if you don't mind, let me alter your perspective before we discuss these matters."

And with Finality saying that, both she and the President disappeared in an instant. And there followed a period of about thirty minutes of absolute silence within that Oval Office. Apparently, there are no telephone calls during this time anyway. I supposed the President gives strict instructions not to be interrupted for any reason during this time of her deliberations and preparations for upcoming speeches or events. The room was deathly silent, and I sat there on that sofa for the better part of their absence like a chastised schoolboy awaiting some disciplinary action from the school principal.

But eventually, the aura of The Room got the best of me. Cautiously and fearing to some extent what Finality might have in store for me if I moved at all, I almost crept around this historical place. If it hadn't been for the gnawing fear that seemed to be my constant companion since this nightmare began the night before in the lab, I would surely have thought I was having a fantastical dream. I ended up at The Desk, which as I said previously seemed overflowing with text-filled papers, charts, maps and a desktop computer indicating that it was turned on and awaiting some interaction, with its screensaver picture of a floating astronaut around the International Space Station. Impulsively, I jiggled the mouse and immediately there appeared on the full screen a spaghetti-like image of some incomprehensible Power Point presentation. There were arrows going in all 360 degrees, from every highlighted heading to every other one on that screen. It was as if its author was unsure what he or she was really trying to highlight, so they chose to avoid any omission by concluding that everything that moves, reacts, sees, hears or smells is related to everything else that moves, reacts, sees, hears or smells. I had the sense immediately that here lies the reason our government and its elected and appointed leaders have become paralyzed. No one wants simply to say that if "A" happens, "B" will be the result. Rather, they cover their precious position of influence, wealth and power by boldly proclaiming that if "A" happens, then get ready, because they are sure "B through Z" is inevitable; and they need more money to understand, protect or avoid it all.

Emboldened by my discovery as a result of this discovery with just the move of a computer mouse, I then decided to shuffle a couple of papers to see what was underneath them. It was at that point, I felt a distinct shove away from the desk, even though no one but me was visible. It was strong enough to nearly cause me to fall over the wheeled arm chair resting behind it. I had been warned. And at that point I hurried back to my seat on the sofa.

It wasn't more than a minute or so later that the President and Finality reappeared, each standing at the oval window looking out into the Rose Garden and still discussing some issue in a hushed tone. Eventually, they both turned towards me, and the President apologetically announced that she was sorry that she shoved me so hard away from her desk. "You looking at that ridiculous Power Point presentation did not worry me. I can't understand either what the author is trying to say. But those papers are "TOP SECRET- POTUS EYES ONLY". I'm sorry if I stunned you."

And for only the second time in that august room, I

spoke in reply. "It was my fault madam President. My curiosity got the best of me. I meant no harm. It was simply curiosity."

"I realize that. And that is why I haven't called security. I realize now that you both have come here with deliberate and life-saving purposefulness. In addition, I know much more than you do about what is at hand and what now has to occur to minimize as much death and destruction as possible. But as Finality, here, has instructed me, only she and I are to know the full story and rationale for what is about to happen. You will be informed by her at the appropriate time.

"So, if you both will excuse me, I have a tremendous amount of work ahead in preparation for what has to be done. I cannot thank you for this intrusion and revelation, Ms. Finality. You have laid at my feet the worst of news, the greatest of challenges and the most meager of hopes for a successful outcome. You are correct in saying that our species has wandered afar from its basic roots and origins, from its humble and ever-aware beginnings. Our arrogance and pride has created a world-engulfing calamity. And if I don't get started doing what you requested, I am sure I will become paralyzed with fear and despair. Your instructions give me a margin of hope. I can only pray there is time left to reverse some of the damage done to this nation and world.

"Please, now, if you don't mind, you need to leave the same way you came in; and do so without raising any suspicion. I trust you will follow-up with the commitments you made to assist me as this process unfolds. Without it, no one will believe me or act upon my instructions and orders.

"That said, I will expect to see you both at noon, on May 15th, three days from now, at the airport in my hometown of Bangor, Maine.   Good day."

THE CONSUMPTION

NINE: THE UNSPEAKABLE BEGINS

There then followed another twenty-four hours of staggering revelations, preparations and a stunning tragedy that brought my life into full focus.

Instead of staying one more night in the hotel, as Finality previously had indicated that we might, we left for Palm Springs immediately after leaving the Oval Office. Reversing what she originally told Finality and I to do, the President personally escorted us out the West Wing door onto West Executive Avenue. She had also called ahead to the Secret Service Office and requested that transportation be provided for us to the hotel and to the airport when we were ready to depart Washington, D.C. As you can image, the looks on the faces of her support staff were stunned, as they shuffled through her appointment schedule for that morning, seeing nothing for the timeframe and then watching her escort us out of her office. For me. it was all becoming so terrifyingly surreal.

Our flight left for southern California at 1:30 p.m. that same afternoon. We arrived in Palm Springs at 7:15 p.m., and I was able to finally get to my own apartment by eight o'clock that night. I was completely exhausted. But as I unlocked the front door, the telephone was ringing, indicating to me that my day was not yet completely over. And as I walked to the cluttered card table that I had the receiver resting on, I glanced briefly at the answering machine. It listed that I had 35 waiting calls! And I don't even have that many relatives and friends combined! Immediately, I sensed that something else was terribly wrong. Everything seemed to be spiraling into chaos.

But before I recount the awful news of that call, it should be noted that upon my departing the airplane in Los Angeles to transfer to a computer flight to Palm Springs, Finality informed me that she would be coming home with me. As she so delicately described it, "we were to become like conjoined twins" over the next few weeks. And you can't imagine how much that news thrilled me: an alien life form who can casually consume human beings becoming my constant companion. And there were no tall buildings in Palm Springs for me to leap off…

So, as I raced across my living room to answer the ringing phone, which of course lying next to it was my cell phone that I forgot to take with me, I directed Miss Finality to the restroom, kitchen or bedroom, wherever she preferred to go. I had already explained that I would sleep on the sofa in the living room/den area. It was only a one bedroom apartment. Eventually, after Abby and Jason's deaths, I sorted my life out enough to move from our rented house to this apartment. My grieving for losing them has not lessened a degree since their car accident, but I was oddly relieved they were being spared this nightmare I was witnessing.

Finality just waved at me as she passed by me heading to the kitchen. Neither of us was able to eat anything on the flight from Washington, D.C. The air was too turbulent, and I just wanted to sleep. I figured that any of her aliens that wanted to invade my sleep at 35,000 feet altitude were especially resourceful and desperate. I had never seen her sleep, however. I imagined it would be nice if the tables could be reversed and one of us humans could invade her brain, where we could spray some alien repellent...

Upon picking up the telephone receiver,, I heard Tom's voice screaming, "Connor!! Is that you?!! ARE YOU HOME NOW?!!!"

In reply, I hurriedly chocked out a garbled, "Yes, Tom, I'm back. What's up? Are you the one who has left all these messages?"

"My God! Connor. It's all an ongoing nightmare. People...even our sleep lab patients... they are disappearing!!"

"What do you mean?" I interrupted. "Are they leaving home and not telling anyone where they are going?"

"No," he stuttered, "It's not like that at all. Nothing so clean or solvable. The patient you saw your last night on duty, the one with the 'stain' as you called it that appeared suddenly during her last REM cycle, she just disappeared the next night from her own bedroom.

"And here's the terrifying part of it. Her bedclothes were left in her bed just like she was wearing them, stretched out perfectly straight, like she was sleeping on her back. But there was not a trace of her anywhere, and she hasn't been seen since.

"But then, that same night in our lab, Kay went in to check on one of her patients after the tracings on the computer screen went completely blank and found that all the electrodes, tape, gel, and her bedclothes were lying in bed just as if the patient was still wearing them, but SHE WAS GONE!! Then she checked the next room and found that BOTH of the patients Kay was studying had disappeared completely!

"Not only that, but Dr. Hildreth just called me at home and told me he is getting reports and calls from his colleagues across the country that the same thing is happening in their clinics and laboratories. And Colleen turned on our police scanner later this morning and heard that the same thing is happening in households across the valley.

"Connor, people are disappearing!! My God, what is happening? Is this in any way connected to what you experienced and caused you to leave town so suddenly? I need to know what's going on. Colleen and I are really scared."

Just then Finality called out to me. "Tell Tom and his wife to come over here immediately. They are not to waste a moment. Tell him to hang up the telephone and get in their car and drive here NOW! IT HAS BEGUN!!!"

Looking fearfully at her, I relayed her message to Tom, who actually seemed relieved at my insistence they come over. And without another word to each other, he hung up the phone, acknowledging, "We're on our way."

I then turned to Finality, who actually almost looked like I had been feeling for the last two days. Rather than her eyes having that steady, unblinking stare, they had begun darting back and forth, as if sweeping the room for a place to hide or escape. And even though her complexion had never shown much color; at that moment she look drained of whatever coursed through her veins. All this probably should have only added to my fears, but by now I was looking for some payback for what I had witnessed and for what I just heard Tom tell me. Little did I realize the ramifications and urgent responses that were now necessary to preserve human life, and quite possible all life on this world, should a feeding frenzy be just beginning.

"What's going on?" I demanded of my captor. "And why do you have the look of someone or something that has sensed the beginning of an uncontrollable disaster? What is happening? What is so disturbing about Tom's message to me?"

"In a word," she began, "it means the process has already begun. They are not waiting for my signal. They sense that I am trying to limit or suppress their insatiable appetites. There has been a revolt, and what you are about to witness is beyond what even the most deranged mind or unbridled imagination could conceive.

"You must pack some food and as much water and liquid as you can into whatever storage space you have in your truck. We have to begin driving back East as soon as we can. It is no longer safe to fly. And we'll need your friends or associates to help us drive. I can protect them as well, as long as they are with us. Anyone else's safety is dependent upon the individual's dream cycling and probably some prayer and good luck."

"What in the world is 'dream cycling'?" I snapped. "You've never spoken to me of this before. Is that something that I should have been doing to avoid having to be your captive? Am I doomed as soon as you disappear? Are Tom and Colleen? Is the President and everyone we see or know?"

"We do not have time to discuss this? Suffice it to say that I would not be taking the time or trouble of being with you if you didn't have some special qualities. And know that I did discuss with the President some implications of it and of what is now unfolding, along with other details that I have not shared with you yet. That will come in time. For now, we must leave. We have a long way to travel in a short amount of time. We must be at the Bangor, Maine airport by noon on May 15th. The President is making her first address at that time. We have to be there and it is impossible to fly now. No one can, except the President. Her aircraft will be secure; I have arranged for that already.

"Hurry, pack some supplies. And if we need a larger vehicle along the way, we will get one. For now we have to use either yours or your friends."

It was sometime round 10 p.m. when Tom and Colleen knocked on my front door, which had been left ajar the entire time since our arrival. In the madness that had followed, securing a door… any door… didn't provide a barrier to the dangers that were mounting by the minute all around us. The horror that awaited every human being on this planet did not use doors; it entered through our brains, by way of our dreams. Even without viewing or hearing what Tom was to tell me, I knew that to be the case.

About this time George, my constant companion up until these last two days came bounding into the room. I had left the front door open. And apparently, Tom had decided to leave George with them. But the minute he entered the room, his mood of joyful reunion with me suddenly changed to one of whimpering and cowering behind me. Puzzled by this never before seen behavior, I looked up from the telephone receiver and saw Finality standing in my bedroom doorway. And then I knew. George sensed the aura of death that emanated from her or it. I tried to reach around and comfort him, but it did little to settle him down. My welcome back to what used to be my little world of escape from the loss and loneliness I had experienced since Abby and Jason's death was becoming unbearable. Fear and confusion were mounting by the second.

And sure enough, once they arrived and Tom began to describe what had happened in the lab, each of the patients who disappeared, including the two whose only sign of their disappearance were their bedclothes and electrode attachments left in place on their beds, arranged just as if they were still in their proper place on the respective bodies. And the recordings, prior to being downloaded, each showed the smudged, circular, vibrating stain squarely in between the two eye channels on the test tracing. Each during REM stage sleep.

Throughout the time Finality and I waited for Tom to arrive, she said very little. Indeed, her mood, appearance and expression seemed to change, even if she wasn't speaking that much. Even George, my very in-tune Jack Russell Terrier, began to be less intimidated by her presence; and he had snuggled up between her legs by the time they arrived. At one point I even glanced over and saw her apparently unaware, reaching down and petting him. Little did I know that it was the beginning of a steadfast friendship: dog and alien. Who would have guessed? It wouldn't have surprised me if Finality had told me that she could communicate with George in some way. My world was unraveling by the second. Talking dogs, combined with mind-invading, entire body-consuming blobs all seemed almost reasonable at that point.

But it was a relief to see Tom and Colleen. Even though we had only really had the occasion to meet and speak in an office setting and maybe a couple of times at a sanctioned office party, the three of us fell into each other's arms as soon as they had entered my apartment. For the next 30 minutes, after I introduced them to Finality, who barely spoke to them afterward, I reviewed as succinctly as I could what had happened to me since I left Palm Springs a day and a half ago. By then it seemed like months had passed since then.

I could tell they were completely overwhelmed and bewildered by it all, and who wouldn't be? Tom, for all his decisiveness in the laboratory arena, became almost mute. It was Colleen who asked most of the questions and seemed to engage me more with comments about the stunningly rapid progression of it all. It wasn't until I made my concluding remarks that Tom finally spoke. And by this time George was now lying peacefully on Finality's lap. I couldn't help but think at that moment that the lambs and hypertensive dogs, such as George used to be, were now lying down amongst lions…

"Is there any purpose in our doing anything? Tom asked with sincere resignation in his voice.

"I haven't the slightest idea!" I blurted out. "I have no idea what was discussed in the private conversation with President Franklin nor do I have any idea what she is going to say tomorrow at noon EST. And I am not getting any indication that Finality, here, is going to divulge beforehand anything that might be said. That meeting, and any plans that were discussed during it, have been off-limits for me to know. I can only presume that at that time everyone throughout the nation will be told what is happening, why and what each of us can do to protect ourselves. For now, what I can tell you is that we are supposed to get on the road immediately and drive as hard as we can, using the most direct route possible, in order that we arrive in Bangor, Maine by noon May 15th.

"And I have no idea what we can expect to see along

the way or what we will see, hear or do once we get there. But, right now, given the gruesome outline of what you have told me is happening inside our laboratory, I would like to get some distance away from here as soon as possible. Maybe this is the epicenter of whatever is happening, I don't know. But, to be perfectly honest, I did see countless of those black forms that I was telling you about when I was made invisible briefly in Washington, D.C. That cannot mean anything good is happening or about to happen elsewhere."

And just then Finality broke her silence.

"Enough of this chatter! You two now know as much as is necessary. We have to be off right away. To delay any longer is dangerous for everyone, including me for the first time in my existence. What is about to happen has never unfolded before… anywhere. A frenzy is about to begin, and we must be off and away. Our only hope of escaping the harvest that is about to begin is to keep moving. However, I am certain there are other safeguards that will protect a precious few individuals scattered here and there, but at this moment I am too uncertain about the future to feel confident that I know for sure. I explained in detail what they were when I spoke with your President. But now I am not as convinced that they will protect anyone. Forces are about to be unleashed that could erase any chance of anyone surviving what is about to occur. Now, HURRY! We have to be off!!"

"Is George going with us?" I asked, knowing full well he had become expendable. But to my absolute amazement, this alien who can perform such pitiless executions and then alludes to worldwide, life-ending events to come, replies that George will be traveling along with us. I thought will odd wonders never cease to manifest themselves, even in the face of possible global damnation. My head was spinning by this time. Getting in a vehicle in total blackness and driving across the starlit desert seemed the best choice we had about then.

I asked Tom if their car was filled with gas, and he assured me that he had just filled it late that same afternoon. We quickly agreed that my old truck was inadequate to the task ahead; our trip would begin using their vehicle.

Once that was decided, I almost reflexly ushered everyone out of my apartment, taking a framed picture of Abby and then, seven-year old Jason and locked the front door. Honestly, I had no thoughts of ever returning to this place. Any future for me that I could envision by this time could only be counted in one-to-two minute intervals.

With minimal conversation once we arrived at Tom and Colleens fairly new, four-door, mid-sized SUV, Finality, George and I climbed into its back seat, and Tom began our cross-country drive of over 3,300 miles to Bangor, Maine's airport. We had about 60 hours before we were supposed to meet the President. There was no way we could prepare for what lay ahead between my apartment and that destination. It involved the unraveling of a civilization.

TEN: 60 HOURS INTO THE ABYSS

I cannot describe the feeling of sitting next to the entity that participated in and foresaw so much of what either was happening or was about to begin.   For the last two days it seemed I ended up sitting beside her, and with her admitted ability to invade my mind and thoughts at will, I was sure she knew every damning thought and feeling I had experienced during that time.   But to her minimal credit, knowing what she did about me, she refrained from acknowledging it.   I had to resign myself that we had another two and half days of sitting next to each other.   I was to share the advent of hell with its lead scout and keeper.

It was a mixed blessing that it was pitch black when we started off.   I didn't want to see anything that might be going on as our ordeal began.   Dawn would bring a cold and terrifying reality to each of us… including even to Finality.

The trip from Palm Springs up and through the high desert region to Interstate 40 was, as usual, devoid of traffic; especially at this time of night.   And once we entered the freeway, even it was less crowded than I anticipated it might be.   My guess was that the terror that was about to reign down on us had not fully taken shape or been fully organized.   Traveling in either direction, there were primarily isolated groups of semi-trailer trucks weaving their way through the Mojave Desert region. Without incident we passed through Needles and were, as it turned out, lucky enough to find a gas station open in Kingman. It was to be our last time to find one open for the remainder of this journey. And it was here, in the seeping dawn light that I thought I might have seen a few darkened shapes darting around some downtown buildings. But, knowing how spooked I was in those early hours of this nightmare, I dismissed it as probably shadows being cast by swinging light bulbs. After all, there was the usual high desert wind blowing through the city when we stopped.

It was also here that we replenished and stocked more food and drinks. Finality had suggested that we should. And I know at this point in this narration that I should be sharing with you some description of the landscape, moonlight and morning sky. But I was just too scared to really notice. This is an account of scratching and clawing survival. It isn't to be a travelogue. Maybe someone else can fill in those details. It won't be me.

And by the time we reached Flagstaff, Arizona, it was of course full daylight, and it was here that our worst fears were confirmed. The darting shapes that I supposed were simply odd shadows in Kingman and Williams turned out to be the all-too dreaded and familiar shapes that I saw while experiencing invisibility in Washington, D.C. And in Flagstaff, all of us in that vehicle began to see some moving freely about the city. A palpable chill seeped through our party when I pointed them out. Each of us, undoubtedly, throughout the course of our trip thus far had naturally hoped that what had been happening in the sleep lab and what Finality had intimated would, did not foretell what actually was going to evolve. Seeing these forms flocking about in this place so far from any major metropolitan area halted those illusions.

From that point we pulled over briefly at a rest stop and Colleen took over the driving, while Tom tried to get some sleep. She became determined to get us out of Arizona as soon as possible. And the rest of us dozed fitfully until she announced that we were approaching Gallup, New Mexico. I suggested we probably needed to get some gas there, but there were no stations open. It was agreed that there were probably some still operating in smaller towns between there and Albuquerque. We hoped that would be the case in either Rehoboth or Continental Divide. But neither did, and we ran out of gas and our battery died simultaneously just outside the community of Continental Divide.

Pulling over to the side of the road, a collective, resigned sigh was heard by all of us. I swear I even thought one escape from George. He had been cuddled uncharacteristically in Finality's lap thus far the entire trip. We'd seen no service stations open since leaving Gallup, and now we were stranded. And Colleen noted that it was exactly on noon, when the President was to be speaking to the nation.

It was then that Tom, ever one of the most aware individuals of events swirling around him I ever knew, spied a number of vehicles and trucks, some appearing possibly stranded, like we were, by the odd way they were parked on the side of the road. As well, he noted what appeared to be a small roadside rest area, adjacent to the freeway. It seemed very odd to have so many there at the busiest time of day and for them to be left in such a haphazard array. You would have thought the State Troopers would have ushered them on their way.

Tom then turned to me and asked, "Do you want to walk ahead and see if we can find some filled gas containers that we could purchase from any of these parked travelers. Surely, someone up ahead will be able to give us enough to help us on our way to Albuquerque. And maybe we can even talk to someone about what the President had to say at noon. I know it would sure help me to know."

And then twisting in his seat and looking straight at Finality, he almost snidely added, "Because I know we're not likely to get much help from your traveling associate."

Still stunned or lost in revere, my captor... both of my conscious and unconscious mind and body and apparently of George's as well, only looked up at Tom and said, "For now, you're right. It is very unfortunate that you were not able to hear his prepared remarks. Maybe someone up ahead was able to record them and will share that recording with you. But, for now, I have given her my word that I would not divulge any of our conversation in the Oval Office or expand on her speech to the nation. Unless you hear the speech or have someone outline for you what was said, you will have to wait until we get to Bangor to have the opportunity to hear what was said and what will be taking place over the next two weeks. For now, your most pressing job is not to find out what was said today, but instead it is to get us to Maine on time."

Tom then looked at me and shrugged. Without another word, he and I got out of his disabled vehicle and began a rather long march up hill to the Rest Area.

Within about 100 feet of our destination, we began to sense that something was wrong. There were no people milling about, going in and out of the restroom facilities or getting coffee at the little kiosk wedged between the "Women's" and "Men's" restrooms. And it was oddly quiet as well. Added to that was a rather sparse number of passing cars and trucks on the freeway.

I cannot tell you what a relief it was for me to have him and Colleen with me. Having them along, unlike when I had to travel to Washington, D.C. alone with Finality, began to give me a confidence to face what unfathomable events or surprises lay ahead. For me, being brave is not something I can draw on if I am alone and isolated; at least not under these totally alien circumstances. I desperately needed someone, preferably someone I knew and trusted, to accompany me into the unknown that lay ahead. Nothing was predictable or familiar. That, alone, robbed you of confidence that you could manage what would come next. With Tom and Colleen along, a determination of some kind began to take hold. I was no longer having to rely strictly on anger, as I tried to on the trip to the nation's capital, to cope and fight back against this dream-world plague.

Our conversation was minimal as we approached the first parked car on the Freeway's shoulder. It was empty, as were the next two and a nearby large truck. But what we didn't take the time to notice was that while they were empty of people; the clothing that they apparently had been wearing was still inside each and every vehicle.

It was when we finally got to the actual Rest Area that we discovered that a few of the cars and pick-up trucks still had their motors running. You kind of expect that will be the case with the large interstate commerce trucks, but not so much with the smaller vehicles. And again, we could not see any heads above the car window sills or dashboards. Likewise, there was no one going to and fro from the Restrooms or milling about the parking lot. There was only an eerie silence.

Taking a deep breath, I told Tom I was going to start

looking more closely inside the vehicles to find out what was going on. He agreed and said he would cross the driveway and examine the cars and trucks on the backside. Almost simultaneously, as we were making our first detailed inspection, we turned to each other and shouted, "There are only clothes in these seats! There are no people!!"

And then it hit me, the blackened forms must have swooped in, like a formation of hungry vultures, and attacked the unsuspecting and sleeping occupants of all these vehicles! Like what Tom described had happened in the sleep lab, where all that was left were the patients' sleepwear and the electrodes, here there were only the clothes the people wore at the time of the invasion.

But why all at once? No way could all of them been dreaming at the same time! What did this mean?

To me, a couple of answers were only too obvious and frightful: the number and size of this invasion is growing exponentially by the hour and as with any expanding swarm mentality and behavior, there are changes in appearances and capabilities. This one was no different. While during the act of dreaming is the preferred avenue of entry into someone's mind and body, with expanding numbers this becomes an impediment to feeding. Sleep in any stage, even drowsiness or paralyzed fright, appears to be acceptable portals of entry if the number of alien beings are concentrated enough.

There is no "how are you?", "we come in peace", nor a "we mean you no harm" associated with their coming ashore, if you will. These conquerers have no intention of getting acquainted, wanting to learn about our ways, habits or virtues. They could care less. We are a food source. Our worthiness as a civilization has become valueless; we are destined to become extinct as a species and possibly as a planet of living creatures... if this hunger continues to grow indiscriminately. The "little green men" that we so eagerly longed to see turned out to be blackened shapes that asked no questions, gave no reasons and took no prisoners.

Something happened to us that became an open invitation for Finality and her compatriots to notice us. And at that moment, with the sight of these empty vehicles, containing only the last clothing individuals were wearing at the time of being swooped up, I sensed the reason for Finality coming to our sleep laboratory, enlisting some of its staff members, having to urgently speak with the President and now going on this awful journey to meet her that's all part of some attempt to lessen the out-of-control frenzy that she anticipated would possibly occur. And it has occurred. Seeing these vehicles convinced Tom and me of that.

I needed to try and get some answers from Finality. More and more she did not appear to be the nexus of evil that I originally thought of her as being. Maybe she really was trying, in her own misguided and predestined way, to save a remnant of so-called intelligent life on this world.

But along with wanting to know what could be the ultimate outcome of this madness, I needed to know if she had discussed with the President why it has begun in the first place. What went wrong with us? Can it be corrected? Do we have time to try? Does she even know the answers to these questions? Or is our existence doomed? Looking out over this Rest Area, I couldn't help but think all was lost.

Just then, Tom interrupted my detachment from the terrifying reality around me of desperately seeking answers to my frantic questions with, "Hey, Connor, come here! I've found a van that appears to have a full tank of gas and there was no one in it at the time of this disappearance. I think we can use it. There is even a gas can in the back for us to siphon gas further on down the line, if we can't find a service station open. Come here quick!"

Running down the rows of cars and trucks to where his voice came from, I saw him opening the side doors of a very roomy van. It had the two arm chair seats in the front and a long bench-style seat behind them. Further back there was about four or five feet of space where we could store our reserve supplies. That area was nearly full of office supplies, with stacks of unopened boxes of bond paper, envelopes and countless other desk supplies. There were even some laptop computers in their unopened boxes.

"Do you think we might need a couple of these computers?" I asked, after doing a mental inventory of the van's interior. "They look like the portable models that already are preprogrammed and equipped to access the internet. We could try to access any news from around the world with them or possibly even send and receive email from the President's Office."

Neither Tom or I had considered bringing a laptop computer along, but neither of us had this kind that was so portable anyway.

"Sure," Tom answered, "it won't hurt to try using them. But we will have to charge them first with the cigarette lighter access port on the van's dashboard. We don't have time to try and find someplace open or take the time to charge them. Grab a couple of the cartons they are wrapped in and let's clear out the remainder of these boxes. We've got to hurry. We're losing valuable time."

Within a matter of minutes we had finished clearing out the back of the van and hurriedly got in the front seats and sped away from this grim place. It was like a graveyard without gravestones. You knew this was the place where countless individuals had their last conscious thoughts and you wanted to pray they had none prior to or during this attack. Throughout this rampaging nightmare, that's the one hope that I have left: no forewarning, no awareness of what is about to happen, no pain and no suffering. Whatever has prompted this mass murder, or execution, as Finality might have justifiably called it, I single-mindedly hoped and prayed for there to be a merciful end to all these precious lives. But, given all that I had seen over these last three days, I resigned myself that I was probably wrong. This was becoming a merciless world.

Due to the lack of traffic at that moment, Tom decided to drive the van back, going the wrong way to Colleen and Finality. It would cost us too much time to drive around looking for any exits or emergency turn-around access roads to get quickly back to them. And within a few minutes he did a U-turn and parked just ahead of his and Colleen's SUV. It was to be the last time they would ever see it.

Unpacking our provisions into the van's rear compartment took another twenty minutes, and then I insisted that I drive for awhile. I also suggested that Finality come up to the other front seat with me. Everyone agreed with my suggestions. Oddly, George would not let himself be separated from Finality's lap. But with some coaxing by me, he did relieve himself while we were repacking our supplies. And come to think of it I had never seen Finality take the time to perform any of the usual bodily functions that we humans had to. Even when we drove back to the Rest Area and all three of us human-types went to our respective restrooms, Finality declined to come with us. Aliens... no wonder they are so weird and bad tempered. They are all suffering from a lifetime of unrelieved retention and constipation.

Just before heading off from the Rest Area, Tom handed me one of the portable computers to charge. Given his expertise and uncanny ability with all manner of computers, I was sure he would be able to glean some usefulness out of them. It was impossible, thus far in our road trip, to raise a radio station on their SUV radio; but we hoped maybe we could get some information from a U.S. based newspaper web site or maybe from an overseas one. We had no idea whether what we were experiencing was a local, national or worldwide invasion. And given Finality's present state of mind… if she even possesses one… it was useless to ask her. Anyway, it was about this time that I scribbled in a very small notebook, in the vain hope I might later prepare something like this narrative: "Can't trust aliens." How's that for insight and an acute ability to summarize? Obviously, my skills as a reporter were rudimentary. I could only hope that they might improve as I practiced.

Soon enough everyone was sleeping, even Gorge and Finality, as I drove the rest of the way into Albuquerque. And honestly, I was glad they were.

For some reason the freeway was almost devoid of traffic, even at this usually busy time of day. It was somewhere around 3 p.m. when we entered the city limits. What I didn't know was that in the President's address she advised everyone who could to begin packing supplies to last at least two weeks. Her address began at 2 p.m. local time and lasted thirty minutes. The city's citizens were still overcoming the shock of whatever she had to say and probably had just begun going home or packing. The mad rush would soon begin. We would be out of the city limits by the time the roadways would become clogged with its citizens, fleeing to the large airport at the edge of their city;

as would be everyone else in the State.

BUT, that didn't mean that all was peaceful and quiet. We expected to see growing numbers of people beginning to rush madly about the city by now. Likewise, in anticipation of this, all available uniformed personnel were mobilized to quell any riots or looting. In fact, in a desperate attempt to avoid such from happening, all citizens were officially deputized by the President during her address to the nation to try and insure an orderly migration of her countrymen and women, one never even remotely imagined before these last few days.

But instead of a mass of panicked city dwellers rushing about, what each of us in that van saw as we dashed through the city on the freeway was what appeared to be almost clouds of blackened forms swooping, running, lurking or poised to attack anyone and everyone. It seemed impossible that anyone could survive their onslaught.

I looked over at Finality, as I steered us through whatever traffic there was in those moments of utter incomprehensibility, and asked, "Is this the way you and your cohorts consumed all the other worlds before this one?"

She replied with a simple, "No."

"What then is the difference?" I snapped. "Were there more or less of you vile creatures? And what's to keep me from swerving this van off one of the higher overpasses and dashing you and all of us to our death? Oh, but I forgot, you appear to be immortal. Your missions are so pivotal to the orderly housekeeping of the Universe that nothing can ever harm you. Please forgive me," I sneered in growing disgust. "You are not on a mission of annihilation; it's one of bringing order back to a wayward world, of correcting some stray customs, or redirecting the course of that world's trajectory…or whatever other pathetic excuse you use when you and your vulture-like beings descend on their unsuspecting and totally vulnerable populations."

"You will not endanger me or this van's passengers," she answered in her steely cold voice. "Because riding in here resides some of the keys to whatever reversal of this process you see taking place around you. And don't be so smug about what is happening. During the course of your world's history, various warring armies and migrations of colonizing peoples have decimated the native cultures that they encountered. Even your earliest hominoid ancestors, the Cro-Magnons, intermingled and championed over the less clever Neanderthals. And certainly the methods these forces and migrations used were most often cruder and more painful than ours; they included swords, arrows, bullets, whips, chains and smallpox versus our use of dreamtime.

"Your native American Indians are being slowly consumed by your culture, even to this day. They may have their reservations, but they are no match for the centuries of conquest and inventiveness that the conquering peoples have imbedded in their psyches. I have looked around in my initial explorations of this world. I see too many of these people languishing in poor health and poverty, despite the governmental handouts. They have been overwhelmed by conquering beings, maybe not as oddly appearing as me and my associates; but certainly you and your kind are having the same effect. It is just taking longer.

"And to answer your first question, there is a vast difference in what I did in other worlds compared to what you have seen me do thus far in this one. I never spoke with the primary leader of a nation before. I never took one of its citizens into my confidence, as I have done with you. And I have never attempted to engineer a recovery plan as your

President outlined an hour ago to this nation and to this world."

"Well, what did she say?" I urged impatiently. "We have a right to know; each of us in this vehicle need to know what we are heading in to. It wasn't our fault we missed her speech. You have to tell us what she said!"

"No I don't," she replied. "It will only prompt more and more questions, and I am exhausted. Leave me alone! You will learn soon enough. It is enough that you get us to our destination in time to meet the President. If you don't, there will be no chance of reversing the process you see playing out around you now. Drive! Focus on the roadway ahead of you. Quit looking about. It will serve no purpose and only divert your energy and concentration away from what has to happen. And that is all I have to say until we reach Bangor, Maine."

And true to her words, that was all she did say until then. The conversation between Colleen, Tom and I went on as if Finality was no longer a passenger. We began to ignore her completely. None of us, we later learned, trusted whatever she said. We were certain we were headed to a certain death. We were just pawns in some cosmic chess game. But there was just enough anticipation and hope that maybe if we did arrive in time to meet Air Force One in Bangor that something redemptive might come from all this loss and death.

But it wasn't long after we left Albuquerque's city limits that the traffic did start to build, with vehicles of all sizes and shapes heading in both directions. Some were obviously trying to escape their almost certain 'disappearance', which became the word most commonly used rather than 'death', 'killed' or 'murdered'. Others, I supposed, might have been praying that these disappearances were associated with the "rapture", a belief held by many across the world. I guessed, either way, whatever they thought, it somehow lessened the horrifying reality that was seeping into every household on the planet. And others were pouring into the city, trying to adhere to the directions given to them during the President's just concluded national broadcast.

However, as we sped along toward Amarillo, with fewer and fewer vehicles zigzagging around us, the freeway became almost our private roadway. Darkness was upon us as we approached the western outskirts of Amarillo. And for miles previous to that there had been no traffic… either way. The desolate landscape was matched by the absolute loneliness and isolation of us being alone for miles and miles. Even lights from farms or ranch houses were nonexistent; our headlights provided the only artificial light. It was as if the world had gone into hiding. And who could blame them. I'm sure if they only knew who or what we were transporting across their landscape, roadblocks would have been erected every other mile to stop us.

Aside from the scattered few cars we passed going through Amarillo, most of which were emergency vehicles, the city was barren. Apparently, as we learned later, all who could were heading toward Fort Hood in central Texas.

And this pattern repeated itself over and over as we raced across the southern tier states through Oklahoma, Arkansas, Tennessee and then up into Virginia, Pennsylvania and New York State. We had to split off Interstate 40 to Interstate 81 about thirty miles East of Knoxville, Tennessee. From that point we wound our way northward through Pennsylvania to Binghamton, New York. At that point we raced eastward onto Interstate 87 which eventually led us almost to the Canadian border, where we exited the freeway system at last and turned east again to Rouses Point and eventually crossed over into Vermont. From that point on we twisted and turned our way through Vermont and into the back country of Maine until we finally reached Bangor.

We preferred to travel at night. Once we entered Oklahoma, the chances of running into some kind of purposeful or accidental roadblock was greatly increased, as were the chances of meeting a military convoy or checkpoint. Some communities large enough to have a National Guard unit, and one that still had enough members available, would attempt to screen any passersby. Even more daunting was when active duty military units would be guarding a section of freeway. Chaos grew with each passing hour throughout the trip… at least until we passed Glen Falls, New York.

Whenever possible, if we became aware of a delay up ahead of us, we would take a turnoff and avoid the congestion. But most often, due to the lack of traffic, there would be no warning and we would suddenly be faced with armed troops. That was when Finality would take over. She never spoke to us, as I mentioned previously, but she would to whoever came forward to check on us. I never heard what was said because of her low tone of voice, but whatever it was or however she said it, we were immediately waved through and a call was made ahead to the next units within that State to let us through.

I asked her a couple of times what she was saying to them, but she only glared at me. Frankly, given my mounting distrust and revulsion at what was going on around us in ever-mounting incomprehension, I simply shrugged off her rebukes. I figured at the pace I was deteriorating, by the end of this journey, I would try to devise some scheme to end her life as well. Just the same, I also realized she could and probably was aware of my every thought and emotion. I was still her captive, in every sense of the word.

What little schedule or plan we had, by the time we reached Tennessee, we knew we were far from keeping it. At the pace we were forced to maneuver, siphoning gas, dodging roadblocks and stopping at checkpoints, we would never make it on time to Bangor.

There were three rather significant interactions between myself and Tom and Colleen over the course of this harrowing drive. And probably it should be noted that we had little other conversation or discussion throughout the journey, except when we needed supplies or more gas. In both these cases we would keep our conversation to a minimum. Who knows why? Maybe it was our seething anger and fright at what was happening and the role Finality was playing in it and how we were such hapless prisoners of hers.

And it should also be noted that our silence during the trip was only broken by our playing music… CD's that is. The one bit of pilfering that we did when we investigated which vehicles had gas in their tanks at the various Rest Areas along the way was to see if they had CD's for us to play. We always left a note when we took them, letting the owner know, if they should return, that we would pay for them. It was the very least we could do under those circumstances. And we played them almost nonstop the entire trip.

Anyway, back to the three episodes that I vividly recall involving Tom and Colleen along the way to Bangor.

The first involved Colleen exclaiming that she was surprised that we were not seeing or hearing any airplane flights, nor did we see any planes land or take off when we happened to pass by any airports. And for that matter we never saw any public transportation, i.e. passenger or freight trains or buses. And in one of the few private exchanges that she had with Finality out of earshot of Tom and I, she was told that it was entirely too dangerous. All terminals, stations and airfields had been closed. The difficulty, as she put it, of others either seeing someone disappear before their eyes or the danger of an accident was too great.

Then one day, somewhere as we were passing through Pennsylvania's back country, Tom asked me when we had one of our few opportunities to be alone together, "There is so little we can do to stop all this, but what say we just surprise this Finality entity by clubbing and then strangling her. Or maybe as a last resort we can find a pistol in one of the vehicles when we are searching for gas. All the cars we enter have keys still in the ignition and we could go into their trunks or glove compartments and search for one."

"Are you crazy?!!" I reacted stunned at his question and remarks. "Don't you know she knows everything that I think or do both in and out of her sight? And she may have that capacity to do the same with you and Colleen."

"Well," he countered, "at least keep our eyes open to an opportunity to do something. We have to try!! Maybe by doing so this entire takeover of our world will be stalled or ended."

I could only shake my head in response. And sure enough, whereas the entire trip up until that point had Finality and I sitting beside each other, when we got back to the van, Colleen was sitting in the front seat next to where I was now driving, and she was in the back seat where Tom was now to sit. And that was the way it went for the rest of the trip.   Tom never drove again.   It was only Colleen and I that did.   There was no more talk of overpowering her after that.   We both knew it was hopeless.   Not only were we physical prisoners; we were mental ones as well.

And finally, there was the most disturbing event of all that occurred as we were frantically trying to race to our final destination toward the end of our sixty-hour time limit. We had only three hours left when we reached the Maine-Vermont border to travel 145 miles before noon on narrow, twisting back roads to Bangor.   So much depended on our getting there to meet the President on time… none of which we were aware of at the time.   Little did we know that our roles in all of this had just barely begun, but if we didn't join up with President Franklin before she began her speech at Bangor's immense airport, total collapse for this country and the world was inevitable.

And to our shock, as we crossed the border, out in the most remote part of the country you could imagine, lining the roadways on both sides to the Bangor's airport entrance, standing form-to-form, with no space or gap in-between them, was an endless line of Finality's brethren!   It was like an honor guard.   It extended up hillsides, along stream beds, across bridges… for endless miles on the horizon, whenever we topped a hill and could see well beyond our present location.   And their eyes tracked our van as we passed; no other movement was ever noted by any of us.

More than even the disappearance of people, this sight convinced me that what was happening to our world was cosmic in origin and far beyond our ability to combat. I saw no hope for survival.   Henceforth, whatever role we were to play seemed futile.   All you could hear from the three of us were gasps of amazement and terror.   The solid black corridor followed exactly our intended route.   In the rearview mirror I kept looking for any movement to occur, but the formation did not vanish or disband. They just kept their stationary positions.

Remarkably, we did arrive at the airport, just in time to see Air Force One make its landing. And we had no problem driving onto the tarmac. The corridor of Finality's troops provided the cleared pathway up to the well-guarded perimeter, provided by active duty and reserve military, National Guard, State, sheriff and local police personnel. And being organized and encamped within this boundary, for a mile in each direction, were masses of Maine's citizens. This was a sight that was repeated over and over for the next two weeks and forty-nine stops. These guarded encampments would shelter the remainder of all the people left in this land. Undoubtedly, given all we had seen prior to our arrival that day, there was a combination of factors that led to these survivors still being alive. Even the presence of the uniformed services did not provide the protection needed to save the remnant of these various States, but whatever was now keeping Finality's vast hoard at bay, it remained so for the time being. "The Consumption", as the history books will eventually describe these last sixty hours, was over. Who knew when or how the next one might begin? For now, everyone left, including us in that van, had come to a prearranged airfield at the command of our Commander-in-Chief. Uniformed or not, we were all to be fighting for our lives in the days, weeks, months and years ahead. Everyone now sensed this. But no one, aside from maybe the President, and most likely Finality, knew how. For now, all the residents left in that State of Maine were gathered within this cordon. All the others were gone. We were in the abyss.

ELEVEN: THE TOUR BEGINS

It was as if each of us, whether those standing or sitting, awaiting Air Force One's discharging the President, or us in the van, which I was frantically trying to slow down as we surged through the makeshift gate on the tarmac, knew that we were all about to be commissioned to battle for and to alter our lives in ways none of us could imagine. Replacing the abject fear, disgust, anger and resignation had to be a resolve.   You could feel it surge through you, once you entered that perimeter.

I pulled the van to a stop where a temporary fence had been erected.   Behind it the President's podium had been constructed.   And just as I did, Finality spoke out loud for the first time since her outburst at me over two days ago.

"Now, listen up!" she began.   "Before we exit this van I need to tell each of you what roles you will have in the days to come.   What I have to say will not be a surprise to your President.   She was briefed by me as to how these next few days would play out and what parts you and I had as they do.   However, I am surprised and somewhat dismayed at the ferocity we have witnessed by my associates.   It is a testament to the sad state of your land and this world that their onslaught has happened so quickly and so extensively.

There is no time to waste in getting the messages we have out to the populace that will be gathered at the places we are flying to over these next fifteen days.

"Do not be shocked at what you see once you climb up on the podium for the first time. Because you did not have a chance to hear the President's nationwide speech two days ago, you are not aware of what has been happening. To you, the traffic we have seen has appeared to head in haphazard directions, as if in sheer panic and with no ultimate direction in mind. But there has been purpose to their travels. Survivors in each State are exhaustively working toward gathering together at the nearest designated airport. And whenever possible, your President advised them to stay within the boundaries of their particular State. What you haven't seen yet, due to the corridor of my companions on each side of the roadway all the way here from Maine's border, is the flow of traffic to this airport. Everyone left alive in this State is here at this moment. And that will be the case in every other airport we land in." (*See APPENDIX: Air Force One's Flight Schedule*)

Hearing this brought a collective gasp from each of us. Still unaware what roles we would be playing in our unrehearsed performance in the ultimate human tragedy of all recorded and unrecorded history, we each looked at the other with mounting anxiety and fear. What could we possibly say or do that might bring some solace or a possible way to escape what by then seemed the inevitable for all of us? And Finality could see the mounting fear in each of our faces.

"There is no way I can dampen the rising concern and worry that each of you has at this time. Much of what you will be saying and doing will come naturally. I will not be asking you to say or do anything that is not already

111

integral to your very nature or work life. For some of you, you are just unaware of your gift or ability. And for others, what I will be asking is what you know better than most in your profession. And most importantly, you know each other. It made this moment easier to bear. And it will make the days ahead for you survivable.

"Now in the short time I have before the President's plane taxies over here to the stage, and she and her small entourage climb up the steps to the prearranged chairs and lectern, I need to outline what each of you will be doing. And I will start with the most straight forward duties first. The more complicated and surprising one will be covered last.

"Colleen, you are first. And your duties are probably the most immediate and vital to the company of us who will be on Air Force One... possibly even to include me. There is no medical staff on board the plane. I instructed the President to limit all the usual personnel who would accompany her. The onboard food supplies had to last these next fifteen days. We would not be having time to restock them once they left Washington, D.C.

"I know you have had experience in both the Emergency Room and Intensive Care Units of various hospitals and major medical centers. Your skills are now needed in a flying clinic. Certainly with the stress and grueling schedule we have ahead of us, your advice and care will be essential. And don't suggest... even to the President. Demand and expect compliance to whatever you say that each of us need to do to stay as healthy as possible. And that includes me. I've never been on an alien world as long as I will be on this one, and I cannot anticipate what effects it will have on me. I must, at all costs, be able to participate in the fifty presentations we will be giving. And it's most vital that I be available once these stopovers are done. It is then the real test comes.

"For, Tom, I need you to explain to the gathered audiences what exactly is taking place when we sleep and what role dreaming or REM plays in that activity. If possible, I need you also to explain a little about the microanatomy and neurophysiology of the brain, as it relates to sleep. I realize there is little time to make any preparation for your remarks, but you will do well. I've noticed during our trip that you are good at thinking and speaking extemporaneously. And if it will help, you can sit back and gather your thoughts while I address my last instructions to Connor here."

Looking squarely at me and lowering her voice, as I turned in the driver's seat to fully face her in the back seat, I became dumbfounded at what she was about to tell me to do.

"In your case, Connor, I must spend more time explaining your contribution to this mission. As you can see, there was this corridor of my associates directing us to this place today. What you did not see is that this airfield and all who are in it are surrounded by them. And that will be the case for all the landing sites we go to over the next two weeks. The urgency of the President's televised message two days ago was intended to spur all survivors at that time to immediately go as fast as they could to one of these designated airfields. The absolutely most urgent ones were here in the upper Northeast portion of the country. My hope was by listing them first the distances and less populated States' survivors could more easily move in the short amount of time allotted them. All people in every State must be in place by the day of our arrival. Each area will be cordoned off one minute after midnight on that particular day. No one else will be allowed in, and any stragglers left are sadly to become fodder for the "stains", as you call them. What guarantee there is of continued existence for anyone on this planet is dependent upon everyone presently alive getting to a safe haven, as has been announced by the leaders throughout the world. Everything that is happening in this country is happening elsewhere. And what is said here will be forwarded by me to those prearranged airfields across the world.

"In the case of every place outside this country, there will be a grace period of thirty days. But if we are not successful in the next thirty days in our outreach and determining a lasting solution to your sad and tragic decline as a civilization, then they and all of you will disappear as well.

"And be forewarned, what you have to say today, despite not knowing yet what I am going to tell you to describe, will only allow all who master and perform the functions a temporary reprieve. What I and each of you have to help me discover is the fundamental reason for this collapse of your civilization to begin with. It is only by beginning to reform, renounce and regain whatever that discovery will entail that a permanent solution to your disappearance will occur. From this moment on we have to be thinking about what that missing link to your continued existence is."

"But why don't you already know this?" I interrupted. "If you have been carrying out these sorts of raids for eons, anywhere and everywhere in the cosmos, why haven't you applied the same solution to those hapless worlds. Surely, you have had to come up with this kind of plan before."

"On the contrary, it has never been necessary before," she replied to my absolute surprise. "This is the most populated and wayward world we have found. Most others of any population have long ago reached accords and found methods to achieve peace and harmony amongst themselves. You obviously haven't.

"And the vast numbers found here has led to the frenzy by my compatriots that you have witnessed on our drive here. I have never seen them so out of control, as they were when our trip began. So difficult was it to control that while I was sitting so quietly and staring so blankly at you and the others, I actually had to transport myself around this country and elsewhere trying to reestablish some order and decorum."

"Decorum! That's a fine word to use to describe the behavior of you and your countless, alien followers." I snapped. "You make this all sound as if there is some kind of politeness or etiquette that must be observed as you liquidate a world's population; otherwise, it just lacks good form. What we observed during and after leaving Albuquerque has been nothing short of a riot and frenzy. I'll never believe anything else. Ever! And I certainly don't and won't ever trust you. Of course, I will do what you tell me to do. What other choice do I have? If I can somehow prevent more terror, like we have been witnessing, I will do my best. But I'll never understand your motives… for whatever you do or say."

"And I wouldn't expect you to," she answered. "The reason I am intervening as I am now is unprecedented. And it is out of character. I have seen something while studying you in your sleep laboratory and in others as I have mingled amongst your citizens. There is something here worth saving. The question is whether it can be done. Whether the missing key to your demise can be found and rekindled. It's a challenge I want to take."

"Like a sporting event," I snidely retorted.

"If you like," she countered. "And for now, I must outline for you what you have to say. Think whatever you will about me and my motives. It is unimportant to me. What is at stake here is the survival of a people, one that I am surprisingly becoming oddly attached to; and coincidentally, you will at least initially, play a pivotal role in attempting to stop what is probably the inevitable.

"What I need you to do, with all the conviction and self-awareness you can muster at this calamitous moment in your world's history, is describe how you dream. After I am finished speaking with you, explore for a minute what you do before you go to sleep. I will want you to describe that process and the details of what you dream essentially every night. And I realize the subject matter you might dream on any particular night does not include all the various subjects you 'preprogram'. But I need everyone in the audiences we go before over these next two weeks to hear the sequence of them. It is the sequencing of your dreaming that is so very important. It is what has protected you from me or any other of my companions from taking you."

"What then is protecting folks like Tom and Colleen, here?" I asked, stunned at what I was hearing.

"My intervention," she answered simply. "But I am unable to extend that protection any longer. My strength and abilities are limited. This is the first time I have attempted this, although I have known that it was a power that I had over my fellow travelers. And my concern right now is that it will become exhausted before we finish our last stopover in California. That is why I have compressed these flights into as few days as possible. Here in the Northeast the states are smaller, and we can visit more of

116

them in one day. This becomes impossible as we move down and outward across your nation.

"And believe me; my voracious colleagues are not happy with me about this stall tactic of mine. They are confused as to why I have not allowed them complete access to everyone here on your world. Time will tell whether it was worth the effort on my part. And if I don't come up with a permanent solution to your potential extinction, the frenzy will resume unrestrained. Right now that is my biggest concern. I know a lot about what has led you to this crossroads in your survival, but I'm not sure what to do about reversing it. In an attempt to find out, when you are flying from destination to destination, I will most likely be searching for the answer. Like when you drove here, just because you see my worldly form, does not mean that I am actually there. I will be searching for answers.

"In the meantime you must tell each audience about your special ability to sequence your dreams. It is this sequencing process that filters, protects and channels your unconscious mind. I have never seen it before, but I don't believe it is simply a gift that only you possess and that others cannot learn how to do. The rarity of it allows you to be protected from the invasive probing of 'the stain', as you call us. Amazingly, through this process you have taken control of your own dreaming.

"Everyone else, and by that I mean, 99.9 percent of the world's population, and anyone else in the Universe as far as I have seen, is not in control of their dreaming. This provides you immunity. Our portal into your mind and body is thwarted. We are unable to invade you!

"But not only do you have that protection, you also seem to be able to resolve personal issues in your dreaming that have been intransigent with others you know and have known.   While dreaming you are able to unite family, friends and strangers, bringing them together in a way that is quite remarkable and as a result strengthens you, the host, from outside influences, anxieties and fears.   And most important of all; it shields your subconscious mind!

"Have you ever discussed this ability with anyone?" she concluded, after confounding me with these observations.

"No.   Never!" I exclaimed.   "This is the first time I've ever heard someone discuss the results of what I do before I sleep at night or day, depending on my work schedule.   I just do what I do because it gives me some kind of lasting peace of mind.   Priming my conscious mind before I sleep with certain thoughts, along with occasional praying, seems to channel what happens when I dream.   But I have never discussed it with anyone.   For all I know, everyone does it.   It was a slow process of collecting the most peaceful and overtly joyous dreaming episodes in a kind of library of possibilities for me to explore during the sleep time ahead that particular day or night."

"Well then," she continued, "it's that process that you use beforehand that I want you to describe to each audience we face over the next two weeks.   I will introduce you and outline the importance of each individual doing this. And I will implore them to begin using it immediately and consistently.   I cannot protect the vast numbers of people out there much longer.   And after we leave each airport, those left behind with have this as their main temporary protection.

"That and one other vital act that you must implore them to use."

"What?!!" I nearly shouted. "You have got to be joking.   I can't imagine what I do has this kind of significance in the scheme of things."

"On the contrary, it is urgently necessary for you to be earnest and honest with everyone you address. And the other ingredient in this protective process is that you emphasize the need to be vigilant when practicing this sequencing process. They must start simply, as you did by steadily adding fulfilling and calming actions or vistas to your individual dreaming. And they must do so every time each day or nighttime's sleep approaches. They must be alert and faithful to this process. And they must be ever-vigilant not to stray from doing it or becoming complacent. If they do, they will disappear, like countless others already have. You have to emphasize how important it is that everyone performs this process continually day in and day out!"

"Does this mean that Colleen and I should do this as well?" Tom interrupted. "And what about you?" he immediately pressed her. "What are you going to do or say to these audiences? Why would they want to listen to Connor and I? We are nothing to them, especially given that the President of the United States has just flown in, and they are witnessing firsthand the extinction process of all civilization!!"

"Oh, I have something to say about all this," Finality cautioned. "And I will certainly make it absolutely clear how important what they are about to hear from you two is worth listening to and doing.

"I have asked your President to make a few opening remarks and then to introduce me, which will include a special attention-getting maneuver on my part. Now gather yourselves. You are about to begin the most important venture of your lives. Dig deep. This is too important to become nervous and muddled. Stay sharp and focused.

We must exit the van now and walk over to where the President has exited Air Force One and is now striding over to the platform. There is no time to lose! We have long days ahead of us."

TWELVE: THE PRESIDENTIAL ADDRESS

It was upon exiting the van that I got my first chance to view the mass of people surrounding us.   While we were being give instructions by Finality, the endless line of her companions hastily filed out beyond the assembled audience to form their guarded perimeter of what inhabitants were left in the State of Maine that 15th day of May.   And as they did, the void was immediately filled with a wordless and soundless surge of survivors.   Their looks of shock and disbelief were soul-wrenching.

I had been caught up in the mechanics of what was taking place in the isolated and incomprehensible days since the "stains" first appeared in our sleep study recordings. And aside from occasionally forcing myself to look out into the scattered farms, towns and cities we passed through getting to Bangor, after leaving Albuquerque, I had focused all my attention on trying to cope and grasp the unimaginable.

A new reality now greeted me as I stepped out of our van.   And along with it came an almost indescribable sense of mission.   The common reflex response of "Why me?" was now useless.   It had tried to surface repeatedly over this last week or so, but now had lost its value as a delaying tactic. Instead, I sensed the advent of another more pressing reaction. Almost immediately after listening to Finality describe what lay ahead for us, "How can I help?" increasingly became my moment-to-moment obsession. The mixture of emotions I had been experiencing since that first probe by Finality in our laboratory, ones dominated by fear, anger, shock and disgust, now merged into ones of conviction and purpose.

I know that I should have probably prayed more for guidance and strength these last few weeks, but over the course of many years that avenue of support and comfort had become somewhat hollow. I never was an especially religious-leaning fellow, even when I underwent some formal theological training. I realize now, it was a feigned attempt to become fully converted to a religious way of life. Whereas, others face misfortune or the loss of their loved ones, whether due to accident, illness, war or a senseless criminal act, with grief, humble resignation and a gradual and graceful transformation before their Maker and those who were sent to reveal this Source of power and love, I turned away.

Seeking answers to the loss of my family led me into a wilderness of doubt, blame and guilt. And no God was inside there for me. I was alone, or so it seemed, and I had remained so up until these last few days. George, my speechless companion, heard my confessions patiently and served as a kind of totem. In all honesty, my actions and beliefs became quite primitive and necessarily visible. I no longer sought comfort in what I could not see or touch.

Then this gruesome invasion of blackened, formless vultures occurred. And at least initially, neither Finality's appearance nor what has followed up until our climbing out of the van in Bangor, had coaxed me to some altar or into a devoutly prayerful response. But they and Finality did fill me then with one abiding thought and obsession: I had to help. Whoever or whatever had brought this horrible reality through our world's ever-welcoming doorway, and was now on the verge of extinguishing us all, had to be combated in some way. And the faces of all those stunned and frightened citizens of Maine convinced me I had to try helping them fight back. Any personal journey of mine as to where God and the Heavenly Hosts existed or who would extend everlasting guidance and comfort would have to wait. I wasn't ready to face those issues yet. But little did I know.

Shaking myself out of this reverie, I looked over and saw Finality lead Colleen and Tom over to where the steps led up to the eight foot high stage; and I quickly rushed over to stand behind them.

The stage had been constructed to Finality's specifications, as outlined to President Franklin that day in her Oval Office. Along with that, Finality indicated that the usual Presidential Seal would need to be mounted on the lectern. In addition, and most essentially, there would have to be a large enough broadcast system to allow whatever was said to be easily understood over a circle, two miles in diameter.

However, she added, that the stage itself was to be positioned at the mid-point of that circle, with the back of the podium positioned along a line dividing the circle in half. Behind it were to be stationed uniformed officers and troops and the parked Air Force One. And she emphasized to the President to avoid any overt attempt at resistance because all along the outside perimeter of the filled semicircle of Maine's remaining population would be an impenetrable wall of her associates. And once our flight departed for the next State in about an hour from then, the other half of that circle, which encompassed the airports runways, would be filled with tents and other necessary accommodations to house and care for the survivors. Food was always to be served out of all the airport's terminals. And this was to be the physical layout for all fifty of the airports that we flew into over the next fifteen days.

I soon became aware that President Franklin's entourage was very small, again at Finality's insistence. They were contrasted by the immense and overpowering presence of Air Force One positioned just feet away from the elevated stage. The plane's glorious markings had to give the citizens assembled before us a measure of hope as well as confirm both the reality and forcefulness of what they were about to hear. Contrasting its presence was the dull overcast sky, with a deepening chill that not only hung on throughout our presentation, but seemed to deepen. That, too, highlighted the ominous nature of what was to be said. (*See Appendix: Air Force One Flying Over Mt. Rushmore*)

President Franklin walked purposefully and erect over to where Finality stood, just in front of us, her three fellow-travelers.

"I see you made the trip just in time to arrive when we did," she began. Then, purposefully ignoring Finality, she turned her head and stared straight at me, adding, "It's a relief to see you again, Connor. I worried about your health and safety after we last met. With all that has happened since we first were introduced to each other, a catastrophe of unimaginable proportions has struck our land… and apparently elsewhere, but I have not had the opportunity or means to comprehensively determine whether other lands and peoples have been invaded like we have. My focus and the limited means available have meant that I focus all my energy and attention into trying to fulfill the instructions I was given in our last meeting.

"No doubt what you have witnessed on your way here over these last few days has been devastating. Just flying up here from the White House has been tragically sobering. I saw lines of people evacuating their homes, as they attempt to meet the deadlines set for being at specific airports in each State. And there is always this awful realization of the disappearance of countless others. Only my rage at all this keeps me focused and willing to comply with the instructions I was given by your captor earlier this week.

"And to you, Finality, have you come up with whatever is necessary for us to have a permanent reprieve from your onslaught? Or are the temporary measures that are supposed to be revealed today the only avenues of escape we survivors have for now? In other words, are we still on a two-to-three week time table for total extinction? And is this pointless charade of gathering all the remaining citizens of this country just a silly ploy on your part to demonstrate to your followers how much influence and power you have to manipulate a backward and, as you noted previously, a wayward people? I want the record to show right at this moment: you disgust me!"

At about this moment I thought that this entire venture was about to go up in flames. I figured, given the terrible potential that this foreign and alien invader and her followers had, that she'd wave her arms and we'd all be consumed in a matter of seconds. I waited without making a sound or taking a breath for her response, as did Colleen and Tom. At that moment I felt that it was unlikely that I would be giving any testimonials this day or any others.

"No, I haven't," came Finality's reply to the

challenges just thrust at her. "I have just informed the three of your people who accompanied me here as to what they would be doing these next two weeks, and that during that time I was leaving the option open for a lasting solution to your survival to be found. As yet, nothing has emerged. But my advice to you, Madam President, is to be careful what you say, both to me and to your audiences. For the first time ever I am taking these extraordinary measures and delaying the likely inevitable only because of what I have noted and sensed both from Connor, here; your most common citizen, and in a premonition I have of the potential promise that lies within your species… one that arose from a much earlier time.

"But there is no time left for us to discuss or argue the matter. Please… lead the way up the steps onto the stage. You will need to introduce me first… after whatever remarks you have prepared. Be ever aware of what you say, however. Do not incite your listeners. My legions are just waiting for an excuse to descend on everyone. All they need is a simple nod from me.

"In turn, I will then introduce Tom and Connor. At the conclusion of their comments, I will then make a brief statement; and you can finally dismiss them and us. Finally, I must prepare you for some theatrics that I sense will be necessary to get each audience's full attention."

"I just hope and pray it doesn't involve any more loss of life," was the President's final words to Finality. And to my knowledge those were her last until we concluded our next to the last presentation in the State of Hawaii and were about to enter California's air space for our very last delivery.

The five of us then filed up onto the stage, which had five chairs already positioned behind the Presidential lectern. No one was to introduce the President. No band was to play "Hail to the Chief". Aside from the stage, there was just a simple honor guard positioned in front of it. Most shocking of all, there were not any sounds coming from the audience as she rose to speak, aside from the occasional coughing one always hears at large gatherings.

And as I looked out over the audience, I was struck by the smoothly shaped hills surrounding us. It was as if the repeated glacial bulldozing was progressively leveling the outcrops of land. Trees tenaciously regrew, grasslands would sprout and wildlife would creep back onto the barren wilderness. But the air of repeated icy transformation held a grip over the landscape. Even now, as I scanned the forested hills, I couldn't help but think that another form of extinction may be at hand. But rather than ice, it would be the darkness of Finality's blackened invaders that silenced self-aware life this time. It made me shudder.

Stepping forward to the microphones lining the front of the lectern, President Franklin swept her head side-to-side, pointedly looking carefully out over the assembled audience of Maine's entire population. There were no shouts or any other signs of recognition from the audience. Formality and overt signs of recognition were now antiquated and senseless.

"Fellow citizens," she began. "I will be forever sorry for having to see each of you like this. Little did I realize at the time I was told to assemble citizens of each of our fifty States like this that there would be such a horrible willowing throughout our midst. I, too, have lost all my immediate and distant family. There is no one else left of my kin except me. Only the will to somehow see that our land and its remaining citizens somehow survive this terror keeps me from losing my mind and determination.

"The one who speaks to you immediately after me is who or what appeared to me within this last week, while her companions began their "harvest", as she called it. It was she, or it, that told me what to say… at the threat of there being total annihilation if I did not. Like you, there is nothing to gain by my being here today. Unless there is some permanent protection found, we will all disappear sometime after the next two weeks. And at this stage in the process you and I will only be given a temporary means to protect ourselves. Up until now our temporary reprieve has been at the mercy, if I dare to describe it as such, of the next speaker you will hear; who goes by the name of 'Finality'. If and when that permanent and lasting solution is discovered or realized, you will immediately be notified. And because our last stop is the Sacramento International Airport in California, the announcement will be forthcoming somehow from there. There is no time to lose. From what I understand, even now our survival is totally dependent on the strength and will of Finality here. If her strength fades, we will be overcome by the alien beings that surround us all at this moment.

"Understandably you may ask, 'why me?' Why am I standing before you now? And I can only surmise that it is because I am the elected leader of this land. I am an authority figure that you easily recognize and one that can mobilize whatever uniformed services that are left intact.

"Finally, I must implore you, even as stunned and horrified as you are right now; be calm, there are uniformed police and troops of various services lined up shoulder-to-shoulder behind me. They will protect you as much as humanly possible, arrange and construct shelters, and feed you from the nearby airport terminal. All lodging is being set up behind Air Force One, just as soon as we leave here.

"But be forewarned, there is now an unbroken cordon of blackened forms bordering the length of the two-mile circle that encloses each of you here, as well as at all the other forty-nine airports where we are to be speaking as well. They are not here for your protection. You must stay here. They will show no mercy if you attempt to leave.

"I do not know if other peoples or nations have been attacked in the same way as ours. After my meeting with Finality three days ago, no transmissions either by satellite, radio, television or telephone were possible outside our nation, except for some limited communication with our overseas military units who I was also instructed to return home immediately, leaving behind whatever material they had overseas. And as far as I know, these addresses that are given at each airport are not being transmitted anywhere else. However, I have been reassured that if there is a permanent solution found to stop our being consumed by these black vulture-like beings, there will be an unmistakable sign that this siege and profound loss of life is over.

"Be brave, dear ones. Find whatever comfort you can in this time of absolute terror. I, myself, am unsure which way to turn or by what means one finds that solace or lasting protection. This invasion appears to be a final act of our becoming extinct. But each of us must have hope. We owe it to all our loved ones that are now gone. And please listen to what the next three speakers have to say. Somehow, in some way, we must prevail. God bless each of you. And may God somehow bless who and what is left of America.

"And now, please listen to what the next speaker has to say."

As President Franklin turned to sit down, there was again no sound that came forth from the audience of many tens of thousands. If possible, the silence was even deeper after her speaking than it was before she began. And by the time she sat in the metal folding chair beside me, Finality had reached the lectern and was leaning forward toward the microphones to speak.

"Each of you, by now, are either so terrified or so confused that you dare not scream out in unison 'who or what are you?', 'how can we trust that you are not some stupid imposter or a gimmick to make us believe that there is hope for our survival?' or 'what proof do you have that we should listen to anything you have to say?' for fear of somehow experiencing the same fate as your loved ones, friends and neighbors.

"I would like to address the last question first, if you don't mind. The answers to the other two can possibly be more readily accepted if I do."

And immediately after she said that, she effortlessly glided from behind the lectern and then in front of it to insure that everyone would have an unimpeded view of what happened next. And before you could blink or turn away, she transformed herself into her native form: that of a blackened form, shapeless except for a bulge at its top end with two very large eyes scanning the audience. It was the same shape and appearance of the thousands of like-appearing creatures that surrounded the audience at that moment.

And then just as quickly, she morphed into a dozen of these figures strung across the front of the stage, and then again she transformed back into the same human form that existed previously but with an additional eleven black figures standing beside her.

Standing perfectly still, each of the forms then spoke in unison without the aid of any microphones. Their voices were as loud as if they were all being amplified electronically. And they shouted, "We are all one and the same. We are who your President calls 'Finality'. And then just as soon as that was done, they each disappeared and standing alone was a single figure of Finality, who effortlessly again glided back behind the lectern.

Sitting where I was, it was clear that a collective gasp and moan was heard throughout the assembled body before us. I even heard the three other individuals sitting beside me do the same... as did I. Who could doubt someone or something so foreign and powerful had come forward, become transformed and was now standing silently before them.

"Next, it probably will be easier to tell you what I am not. I am not a messenger or some kind of a savior. I am nothing so bold or grand. Nor do I stand here simply to issue you a warning. You have had all of those that any world could reasonably expect to get.

"I and all those who surround you or who have caused the disappearance of so many among you can best be described as cosmic vultures or buzzards. We feed on the corpses of civilizations that have deteriorated due to prolonged strife, wars, greed, selfishness and the inability to establish ways to govern themselves humanely and peacefully. There is the scent of death that brings us to a world like yours. And our appearance signals the immanent end of a particular world's dreaming inhabitants. It is the easiest and most efficient way we have of removing or eliminating your kind. It is the portal for our invasion, and there are literally billions of us now occupying your world. And, like so much that happens in the natural world, the innocent suffer along with the guilty. That is why you were given many thousands of years to learn, to reason, to celebrate and to find peaceful solutions to your problems and differences and then to establish a just, free and gracious civilization. Now that these goals have not been met, all have to suffer equally.

"But why have each of you been spared... at least up to this moment... you might ask? Simply stated, I halted the process. I alone can do that. But it is not an unlimited ability. And I have never done it before. Once I give the order to halt, there is only about one month in your time before the process of disappearance will begin again. And I will not be able to stop it. Nor will I want to.

"How then does this failed evolutionary process occur within a civilization or world, such as has happened to yours, you might ask? Essentially, it is through a process that I call 'tampering'. And I describe it as involving willful and prolonged deception. You earthlings have been deceiving yourselves about the abuse of your bodies with drugs, hedonist pleasures, gross obesity; about using outlandish and impulsive rationalizations for your deserving entitlements from governmental agencies or from others around you; and about a remarkably distorted sense of privilege by so many who are or were gifted or were blessed. Further, many of you deceived yourselves about how you could abuse and enslave others through acts of intimidation, terror and homicidal chaos. And most recently in your planet's history, you have begun deceiving yourselves with scientific exploration into reproduction, genetic alteration, selection and exclusion. Your tampering with the natural world around you and with yourselves has reached a point that my associates and I could not avoid the scent of putrefaction rising from this planet.

"And by your leaders and enough of your citizens tampering, it eventually led to the entire population becoming infected to some degree with its effects. And by doing so, it left you vulnerable to our attacks. Only the most precious few of you have had the time or presence of mind to master the process of sequencing your dreams. And by some stroke of possible good fortune, I happened to appear in a laboratory before one person that actually performs this activity on a daily basis.

"Pay attention to what both of the speakers say after me. The first one will acquaint you with what dreaming is about and its internal origins and extreme vulnerability to damage or invasive intrusion, such as what happened with me and those who surround you now. This pause in our onslaught is due entirely to my halting it in the hope this is a process that you will start practicing this very night. Any of you who don't will become immediately vulnerable to attack. And unless a permanent solution is somehow found beyond it, all of you, including those on this stage will vanish by the end of the month.

"I will now introduce two of the individuals sitting behind me. They have no weighty credentials to address you on this occasion... but for that matter, neither do I. The era of over-inflated resumes is over. Tom, the first speaker, will describe the process of dreaming and its origins. And the second, Connor, will outline for you the two avenues for your temporary safety: diligence and dream sequencing.

"Again, I repeat, they are only temporary solutions for your survival. Somehow, someone will have to help me and you discover a permanent means of protection from our eager presence and appetites. In one month from this day, it must be found. In the meantime, DO NOT ATTEMPT TO LEAVE THIS PLACE! It is only here that contact with you will be possible should something hopeful be realized or discovered. You are surrounded, and you will remain so, whatever the outcome, up to a month from now.

"Now let me introduce to you Tom Rhodes. He will outline the architecture of sleep that incorporates the actual process of dreaming. And for your information his wife, Colleen, who is sitting beside him, will be our medical officer for the next month. Her role in all this is likewise pivotal. If any of us become ill or incapacitated, there is no chance of our success or of your survival. Here's Tom. Listen carefully to both him and then to Connor Pruitt who will follow."

I could now sense a restlessness sweeping though the throng of people. Finality had not given them much hope for the future, and certainly with Tom and I having absolutely no credentials or notoriety, they had to be thinking why listen to us? Tom glanced over at me before he rose to speak. The look on his face confirmed what I was feeling. And neither of us had any time to prepare our remarks. We were going to have to speak strictly from personal experience.

Little did we know that after we were introduced by Finality, she slipped behind our chairs and stood at the rear edge of the stage. Apparently, when she gave President Franklin the dimensions of the stage, it had to have about ten feet more space behind the metal chairs we were using to its back edge. It was in the middle of that space she stood and transformed herself again without any of the four of us being aware. But certainly everyone before us was, and their restlessness was immediately halted and deathly silence gripped the entire audience. There was not a cough or sneeze heard throughout both our presentations.

Why? Finality had transformed herself again, as we

were later told by Air Force One's crew, back to her blackened form; but now it stood over twenty feet tall and her huge eyes swept constantly over the audience while we spoke.

THIRTEEN: TOM AND CONNOR SPEAK

Again Tom looked nervously at me as he rose to speak for the first time. It was highly unusual to see him this nervous. He seemed to have an innate ability to meet unforeseen circumstances or problems with an uncommon calm and steadiness. I, on the other hand, seemed to take every opportunity I could to get nervous and worry, particularly with new or unexpected ones. I was so relieved he was the first to speak. He began by clearing his throat and just scanning out across the mass of upturned and deathly silent faces. Not even small children or infants were talking or crying. It was as if, like newborn animals in the wild, sensing danger and threat, they huddle silently to lessen their exposure and that of their parent. Then Tom began.

"Because I have been commanded to speak to you about sleep and dreaming, I will rely to a large extent on what our sleep laboratory's medical director has taught me and my staff over the years. I only wish he were here, instead of me, to present this material to you. I will try my best to make it as clear as possible. First, I want to begin with the functional anatomy of the brain, the focus of where this invasion Finality and her legions of killers make their entry and eventually perform their murderous acts.

"Imagine resting before you on an exam table is a human brain; one that has been removed from someone who has recently passed away and donated their organs to science and medicine. Immediately, you are struck by its size, shape and spongy-appearing convolutions which course over its entire external surface. And when you look at it from its front or top, you notice a prominent gutter or fissure that runs its entire length, dividing the brain into two hemispheres.

"What you are seeing are the two cerebral hemispheres. They appear, on a side view, to roughly resemble a large mitten, with the finger portion being extra thick and the thumb portion being equally large and puffy. At the front of this mitten is the prefrontal lobe, where, for the lack of better explanation, your ability to acquire knowledge or learning occurs; and it is here that your coordination using skilled responses takes place. It allows you to develop mature, anticipatory behaviors. At the rear of this mitten resides the sensory centers and more specifically for our purposes here today, it contains the visual cortex.

"Now if you did two rather dramatic, investigative maneuvers with that brain, you would be able to observe the two centers that are pivotal for exposing where these invasive aliens that now surround us make their entry into us.

"First, on the underside of that intact brain are seen the large optic nerve fibers at the front of the brain, with the eyes possibly still connected to those nerves. And the place where the two optic nerves meet, and actually crisscross our eyes respective visual signals, is called the optic chiasm. Immediately behind that intersection is where the hypothalamus is located. This area is called the midbrain, an area nestled between the two mittens we observed earlier.

"The hypothalamus is where light is first processed by the brain and where our diurnal rhythms, or sleep/wake cycles, are activated and controlled. In other words, when you become sleepy at the end of your work day, it is from here that you are receiving indicating signals that you need to get some rest. Its fibers are extremely prone to any injury or damage, and this is one of the focal points for our invaders entrance into our bodies.

"The second and more likely area that the actual, destructive invasion by the 'stains', as my associate Connor behind me describes them, takes place is in the limbic lobe of our brains. To view that structure, you would now need to separate the two hemispheres or mittens of the brain and examine the interior portion of one of these halves. Immediately underneath the spongy mitten area on this interior surface you notice a more solid-looking formation. It is the limbic lobe.

"Within it there are two major organizational components: one promoting functional attributes and one leading to dysfunctional. Incorporated within its functional responsibilities are motivation, memory, the sense of smell, instinctive responses and emotional style or tone. Its dysfunctional responsibilities are fear, frustration, anger, rage and violence. And for our purposes, the most important area we need to explore even further to understand why the particular mode and time of day is chosen for these invasive hordes to attack us is the limbic systems' memory function. For within it specially dwells the hippocampus, a 'seahorse' shaped structure.

"This is the most vulnerable structure in the entire brain! Any loss of oxygen immediately begins affecting its seahorse-shaped structure. And within this section lie large, pyramid-shaped cells that are active 24 hours a day. They are most active when we are dreaming, due to their much higher metabolic demand during this period. They serve as a kind of beacon for our invaders. And without question, these particular cells are the most vulnerable of structures in our brains. And it is here the 'stains' strike us first.

"Saying this, now leads me into a very brief description of the structure or stages of sleep and what in particular happens during the period of time that we dream. And finally I will outline what we are measuring when a sleep study is being performed. Handouts have been made available for you to follow that aspect of this portion of my presentation. (*See DREAMMARE's front book cover*)

"Sleep is distinguished by having two primary divisions: Rapid Eye Movement or REM sleep and Non-Rapid Eye Movement (NREM or non-REM) sleep. Furthermore, NREM is broken down into three stages: N1, N2 and N3. There are measurable and non-measurable features occurring during each of these three stages. The measurable events are found on your handout; those not quantifiable are primarily psychological and neurological, which are usually revealed in an individual's sleep diary or post-sleep test questionnaire. Sleep normally has three to five full cycles during a given night. Each cycle's usual sequence is from N1→ N2→ N3→N2→REM. And each of these complete cycles last anywhere from 90 to 110 minutes.

"In an attempt not to overload you at this time of your grieving and confusion about the staggering events unfolding around you and me, I will not go into detail on the specific features with each stage, with two major exceptions.

And they both involve what occurs during REM sleep. The first is that upon entering this stage, it is highlighted by rapid eye movements (seen on your handout at the top of the page and interrupted by a black smudge or 'stain', as my associate, Connor, has described it). This is seen on your handout on the "LEOG" (electrooculography) and "REOG" channels. The second is that once this stage is entered, which comprises about 20%-25% of your total sleep time under normal circumstances, skeletal muscle atonia, or loss of active muscle tone, is immediately experienced. This too can be seen on your handout on both the 'chin' and 'Leg EMG' channels; there is no activity noted on either. You are essentially paralyzed during dreamtime.

"As mentioned earlier, I will note as well the other channels that are seen in your handout. 'Body' indicates whether the individual being studied is lying on her or his right or left side, the stomach or on their back. 'C3A2', 'C3A1', '02A1' and '02A2' represent the brave wave signals from the right and left cerebral hemispheres or 'mittens'. The 'chin' electrodes monitor muscle activity associated primarily with snoring during obstructed breathing episodes and with the atonia seen in REM. The 'ECG' electrodes monitor the individual's heart rhythm, and the 'RR' record the heart rate. It is not uncommon for individuals who have certain sleep disorders to have their heart rates and rhythms change dramatically during sleep, especially during REM. The 'Micro' channel picks up snoring events. The 'Flow' channel allows someone to identify when the flow of air into and out of the lungs is impeded or stops, as in sleep apnea. The 'Chest' and 'Abd' channels display the muscular effort an individual makes to take a breath. The 'SaO2' channel displays the arterial oxygen saturation at any given moment. It will rise and fall depending on any breathing obstructions, heart rhythm abnormalities or due to factors not readily identifiable. And finally there is 'STAGE', which indicates which of the four sleep stages the individual is in during this 60 second cycle.

"In summation, by my noting where the most vulnerable structure is in our brains, explaining that REM is our most vulnerable stage of sleep and finally that we are paralyzed during dreaming, you now see the profound weaknesses we all share, which Finality and her followers have capitalized upon with their terrifying invasion and our mass disappearance thus far.

"The handout you have before you is a copy of our laboratory's first indication that something was amiss. None of us, including our Medical Director, had ever seen such an aberration. And it ultimately led to the disappearance of that patient, like has happened to millions of our fellow citizens. This particular 'stain' you see on the handouts, represents the first contact anyone had with these invaders. It transformed itself into being Finality, the entity introduced by President Franklin and who first met Connor in our sleep laboratory five nights ago, when this invasion began.

"To combat this invasion, we have to have some means of delaying their entry into our most vulnerable anatomical structure, our brains, and at our most vulnerable time, when we are dreaming. To do this, I yield now to Connor, who I hope will give us the key to that defense."

Honestly, in retrospect, I had had no time to prepare any remarks. And I am absolutely miserable when it comes to speaking extemporaneously. Following Tom's fine outline of sleep and his having a handout, which I had no idea was available, but apparently Finality had at sometime alerted him to the fact they were being distributed, I was flustered. Actually, I'm sure I appeared to be staggering to the lectern to speak. I had no idea how to begin or what to say. I was humiliated.

And yet, just as soon as I rose to approach the lectern, I glanced back to see the looming transformation of the much smaller 'stain' that appeared to me in the laboratory that night, and a resoluteness seized me. Finality's huge eyes staring down at me, as her massive head leaned forward, was enough to force me into a fighting mode. Whatever I had to say had to be forceful and helpful to the survivors of this never-ending horror. Becoming more erect as I walked up to the microphones, I leaned into them and spoke.

"My name is Connor Pruitt, and I was instructed by the huge form standing behind me to tell you about what I do each day or night before I slip off to sleep. Apparently, whatever there is about this process protects me from any invasive acts by her or her cohorts. All I can credit that to is that, somehow by doing this, it boosts a mechanism within these most sensitive brain centers that Tom has described and in which neuroscientists are now discovering to be our brain's 'default mode'. By doing what I will soon describe to you, it appears to enhance a sweeping, protective mechanism against 'foreign' invasions of stray thoughts and dream cycles. The dream center becomes preprogrammed and preoccupied with the particular material I supply it before going to sleep.

"However, the immense black form hovering behind me has been quick to add that this ritual that I perform before I sleep can only be a temporary deterrent, but that it will at least provide you protection for the next two or three weeks. However, you must be diligent and persistent in performing it, and you must instruct you children to do the same. Vigilance and the dream sequencing methods that I will soon outline for you will stabilize our current loss of life, provided you practice it faithfully. I have been assured of this. And at this point what else do we have to protect us against these unknowable and vastly overwhelming invaders?

"I have never thought of or described what I do before I sleep as 'dream sequencing', but that is the term that has been adopted by Finality who now stands behind us. Practicing this technique appears to allow my dreaming to resolve intransigent personal issues; reunite and find comfort with people I know, have known or desire to make peace with; shield the unconscious mind from danger and threat and strengthen the host for the day or night ahead, depending on the time of day when the period of sleep is initiated.

"Basically, it involves preprogramming your brain before you go to sleep with visions of people you know, knew, love or loved; visually imagine places that have particular meaning, whether they are real or not; reenact various activities that give you the greatest comfort and peace and finally recall any past dreams you have had that have included these themes. By doing this, you are downloading enough material into the brain that during the time you are most vulnerable to invasion by the 'stains', there is no opportunity for them to gain entrance. The dream sequencing is too tight, too involved and too much under your unconscious control to allow them entry.

"Examples of visions that I use and that have reoccurred over the course of my practicing this have been having relatives express tenderness and love toward me... something I had never heard or experienced from them before; instances where I express the most heartfelt emotions to others; times when I revisit a beautiful shining light radiating from behind snow-capped mountains; moments when I stand on a hillside singing in a voice so pure and loud that it rings across the entire world or periods when I recall the words or particular note quality of the song, ones which I have never heard before; soaring and flying under my own power; and finally walking in a heavily wooded area, surrounded and comforted by immense trees or being in the comforting presence of someone of great beauty and grace.

"And let me hurriedly add that it was apparently by chance that I began practicing this process. It stemmed from my simply wanting to reexperience what had been a 'sweet' dream, as I used to call them. Now I have been told they are a means of protection, albeit temporary.

"All I can do at this point is encourage you to practice what I have described. And obviously, if you are prone to praying, please continue to do that as well. Incorporate whatever aspect of your prayers and experiences surrounding your religious devotion... provided it is positive and uplifting. This is not a time to inject doubt, fear or disappointment. You want your brain to be at peace for this process to work. And when it does, during the time of your longest dream cycling, you will experience the joy of having reoccurring dreams that are most welcome and for our purposes... protective.

"I wish all of you the very best. And I wish I could do more and that this process would give you and me lasting protection. We can only hope, and those of you that do, pray that a permanent solution will be found for our safety and continued existence."

Then as I turned to sit down, I almost bumped into

Finality, who by this time had returned to her more pleasant appearance as the younger woman I first met on the airplane. She apparently wanted to follow up with a summation of some kind before the President adjourned our presentation and quickly moved on to the next airport. We still had three more assemblies to address before this day was over, and our next stop was the Edward F. Knapp State Airport in Montpelier, Vermont. As I was just sitting down, she leaned into the microphones and spoke.

"You must quickly process and apply the information you've just been given. Frankly, the content of Tom and Connor's presentations has surprised even me. It again demonstrates the hidden abilities and resources that lie within you as a species. I wish I could assure you that what they have said, coupled with whatever permanent solution might be discovered, will be enough to give you lasting survival. But I can't. I will promise you, however, that in the next two weeks I will make every effort to find some recourse or avenue for permanence. Believe it or not, I sincerely and honestly want that for those of you still left in this place.

"But I've just learned that even now my overly-eager associates have begun taking countless lives throughout your world. The absolute end of humanity is beginning. If we don't find a way to sustain your lives, soon you, too, will begin disappearing because of those who now surround you at this moment.

"We will not be able to return here to give you the hoped-for news that a permanent solution has been found. And, of course, there is no capability left to broadcast messages nation or worldwide. All widespread communication, aside from direct contact like this you are just witnessing, is no longer possible.

"The only way you will know you are safe will be if and when those of you living on the perimeter of these enclaves at the fifty airports across this nation notice there are no longer my companions guarding you. They, themselves, will have disappeared. Only then will you know you are free, but I'm sure that freedom will require some special and dedicated change in your behaviors, attitudes and actions... forever.

"Now, we must go. There is so much to do. Your President will now speak."

It seemed to me that no one in the audience had taken a breath throughout the whole time we had spoken to them. And it was only when President Franklin rose and came forward that a kind of collective sigh was heard. Probably it was due to their seeing and hearing from someone they recognized. Due to the need to push on, her message was short, but her voice was filled with warmth and compassion.

"Take to heart what you have heard and seen this day. No one could have predicted this desperate calamity surging around, over and inside us. Find whatever peace you can in the days ahead. Pray if that gives you comfort. Stay calm and hopeful. We must. Like you, I am overwhelmed at what has happened, and I have no idea what might afford us a permanent solution to this onslaught. But be assured we will be in physical contact with all your fellow citizens across our nation and will continue searching and groping for the permanent solution these next two weeks. May God bless you and the United States of America. Therein, somewhere lies the answer to our ultimate survival."

That night, for the first time in weeks, no one, not one individual disappeared in the State of Maine. And all her citizens' dreams were enchanting, or "sweet" as Connor described his.

PROVIDING COMFORT AND SEEKING A
PERMANENT   SOLUTION

FOURTEEN: FORTY-NINE AIRPORTS TO GO

There was no pomp or ceremony as we all stood up and descended the steps onto the tarmac and walked back to the ramp leading into Air Force One; nor was there any forthcoming from the other three destinations that day in Vermont, New Hampshire or Massachusetts.   Each audience that day, as we flew in and out simply stood in mute silence.   It was like they were all shell-shocked; like they were already weary from endless, battlefield warfare, even though their fight for survival had only just begun two to three days ago.   I could only image the collective effect of this silence that would be greeting us over these next two weeks.

And it had to be my wanting some visible change to occur, or more likely just my progressive fatigue beginning to take effect, but it seemed by the end of this first day's announcements that Finality appeared slightly more "human", if you will.   She seemed drawn to President Franklin and Colleen for conversation or possibly even some comfort or reassurance.   But on second glance, I knew I had to be wrong. The Empress of Extermination could not possibly show some weakness or have some reservation about what had been hers and her companions' sole mission throughout infinite time. Still, I made it a point thereafter to be more overt and dedicated in observing her as closely as possible. I wanted to see if there were weaknesses that may emerge or opportunities for taking more control of our desperate situation, if she should become less attentive or more trusting of us. Maybe those poor and desperate folks huddled below us at these airfields were surrounded and helpless, but I felt that those of us in this airplane had an obligation to try and fight back, get even or at the very least show that we didn't lie down pitifully at the end of this ordeal.

And the other observation I made, but only tentatively and reservedly, was that Finality appeared somewhat fatigued by the end of that first day; like she was having to expend great amounts of energy to maintain this process of holding her associates at bay. She did admit to me at one point when we were flying into the Westover Air Reserve Base in Springfield, that she was thankful, if she had even the slightest right to use that word, that we were now in the process of telling all the survivors about Tom's and my temporary measures for their survival. She intimated that each time an audience was told, she could relinquish her power to hold off the 'stains' that surrounded them. The audiences at that time then had the knowledge and ability to fend them off... at least temporarily.

As we filed off the stage after that first presentation, President Franklin led the way, which was cleared by an assortment of uniformed personnel, representing local, state and national agencies and services. She had requested in her national address that all uniformed personnel who had survived the initial onslaught, of any service, begin wearing their uniforms whether on duty or not for the remainder of the next few weeks. This was apparently not something Finality had suggested, but our President wanted that identifiable presence in the background at each of the airports. She thought it might provide a sense of security and order for the days that followed, in which there would be very little of each.

Once we climbed the ramp and entered Air Force One, she again took command and led us to the area that would be our quarters. Immediately, Tom expressed his surprise to me that we were entering the same doorway used only by the President and her family. We were entering into the middle level of Air Force One and were escorted by President Franklin to the area usually reserved for the reporters on that level, except no reporters were on board for this flight or for any of the others.

Any documentation of what preceded or happened throughout these next forty-nine remaining destinations was to be left strictly up to me to record. And apparently the reason for that was that I was initially the first contact person. Despite my objections, this had been a unanimous decision by our small number of dignitaries and travelers.

Not surprisingly, for national security reasons, no one outside a select few was ever allowed to see or know about what Air Force One contained or how she was organized. We four weary travelers from Palm Springs were to become the first exceptions to this order. We had complete access to all areas of the plane. But we naturally stayed away from most of them. Colleen spent a lot of her time, when we were not in the various airports, in the medical facility, familiarizing herself with its contents and capabilities. There was not the usual medical doctor onboard. None could be found alive before their flight departed from Andrews Air Force Base that morning for Maine. It almost seemed as if the 'stains' targeted certain individuals and occupations in their initial onslaught.

Tom, Finality and I spent most of our "free" time in the President's Office or in the onboard Conference Room, when we were not sleeping in the cabin section reserved for reporters; an area I might add that easily compared to the First Class Section of most commercial airplanes. And all of us ate our meals in that same conference area.

The others on board that day, excluding President Franklin, included the flight and reduced cabin crew, one aide to the President and a small military contingent representing each of the services. These individuals were to carry all the ceremonial flags up to the front of the stage at each airport. And with them were two non-flag bearing personnel who carried loaded weapons. It was felt that somewhere along the route restlessness or panic may be a problem. And Finality emphasized over and over to President Franklin, no matter the danger or slim window of time available, how important it was that the survivors were addressed in each State. We had to have some onboard protection to ensure this.

The total personnel flying off from Bangor that day included the President and her aide; four flight crew members; five service members of the Army, Navy, Marines, Air Force and Coast Guard; two armed escorts; one individual who carried the State Flag where we landed; two individuals who cooked and did minor housekeeping chores; two airplane maintenance personnel; two communication specialists and the four of us from Palm Springs. It was a total of 24 occupants to be housed onboard Air Force One for the better part of a month. In fact this particular air plane has the capacity to hold 2000 meals. And projecting that the 24 of us ate 72 meals a day, we calculated we had enough food on board for 27 days without having to restock. The President felt it was an ample supply. We each knew our mission would be finished, one way or the other by then.

One final note as we took off after that first stopover in Bangor. The pilot had already discussed with President Franklin a maneuver that he wanted to perform as we departed each State's airport. It was to be a signal of support and recognition of their presence and value. In short, it was to honor them. Once he and the copilot got the plane up to about five thousand feet elevation, they circled the enclosed area, filled with the guarded survivors, then flew off to the north about five miles and turned and came as low as they safely could and gave the traditional flying salute to all those below us: dipping each wing as we flew by.

From what I understood later, it was a hugely appreciated and acknowledged salute by the President and our nation. It signaled both recognition of their plight but also said we had resolve and the will to survive. We were all together. Our band of citizens was united in the fight that lay ahead.

And this first time as I looked out the window, I saw the most remarkable sight. Below us, as we flew in the wide circle and then made the pass-by salute, there were tens of thousands upturned heads, with arms waving, hats being tossed into the air, and mouths open in shouts of determination. Surrounding them was the impenetrable black wall of Finality's devil creatures… standing mutely and motionless. It was a contrast of seeing those with hope and those who represented despair and death. Each of us onboard the plane who witnessed this sight responded with our own yells of support. It was spontaneous and happened for each of the next forty-nine stops.

Finally, we finished up that first day's four presentations by 10:30 that night. Following the last one, President Franklin and Finality decided to have the flight crew secure Air Force One, and we would leave the next morning at daylight for the next day's scheduled stops. Understand there was no electricity being generated by this time... anywhere. Any runway lights were to be provided by smuge pots bordering the runway, if a landing or departure had to be made in darkness. And that was the case for our landing in Springfield. This decision to stay in place overnight was greeted with relief by those citizens drafted into being the temporary ground crew and by our own flight crew. Our personnel were all sound asleep by the time we returned to the plane after that fourth presentation; and unbeknownst to me, each was now practicing dream sequencing. President Franklin insisted that they must.

The next day, our second of these four-a-day meetings, began at dawn. And the emblem of national resolve lifted off and left for Providence, Rhode Island at 7:00 a.m. sharp. Our presentations this day were identical to the first. And like the day before, each audience was deathly silent before, during and afterwards. Only when we flew over each one, giving them our heartfelt salute with Air Force One dipping her wings in our, by then, traditional bypass wing-tipping maneuver, did we see animation and some signs of hope and determination. And again, we spent the night at the Harrisburg International Airport, our last airport destination for the day. All of us on board the plane were tired; and to push on to Frankfort, Kentucky, in the growing darkness seemed senseless. And it was a good thing that we waited.

Going forward over the next two weeks there was an almost monotonous routine that began to develop. I say 'almost' because the circumstances of our making these multiple stops were anything but casual, as were our most urgent messages. I guess it is just human nature to see something done repetitively, no matter the life-saving quality it has, as routine. Oddly, I began to sense myself taking on more of a leadership role in this process. And it certainly was not my intention or retiring nature to do so. It appeared to be happening by some curious design and by some unmistakable default. But I get ahead of myself. Because it needs to be noted that five, very distinct incidents occurred along the way; and in the case of the last one, an earth-shaking one at that. And as the appointed chronicler of these times, I must describe them for any and all who may follow us. The fifth one, in particular, must be recorded and then remembered by each of us forevermore. The first one occurred on Day Three of our journey across America.

FIFTEEN: THE FIRST FOUR INCIDENTS

No routine had been established by the third day of these stalling stopovers, which were in all likelihood only postponing the inevitable. But it wasn't until we reached the Richmond International Airport in Richmond, Virginia, that we realized all too soon that our silent and patient receptions could not be taken for granted any longer. By 6 p.m. when we landed and disembarked in Richmond we were not greeted with overwhelmed and frightened citizens, their voices muted or silenced with resignation. The time of everyone's, initial shock and resignation was starting to be replaced with something more direct and useful... but, more likely, very dangerous. There was continuous shouting coming from the assembled audience, the largest one we had to speak to up until then. Expressions of doubt as to reason for our coming and what we had to say were being voiced throughout the throng. We were not in an especially dangerous situation, certainly not as much as being in the clutches of those who surrounded this audience. But the assembled mass could become unruly and uncontrollable if we were not cautious about what we did and said.

As we assembled inside Air Force One to exit its

open doorway onto the tarmac and walk the few feet over to the usual elevated platform with the lectern and microphones already arranged for us, Finality called out to President Franklin.

"I'll speak first, if you don't mind, Madam President."

It always amazed me how Finality addressed and even showed some surprising deference to President Franklin. When you are the Vulture Queen of the Universe, you'd think that she would have no respect for anyone. She certainly showed me and the other travelers none. And of course, it probably doesn't bear mentioning again about her calloused treatment of strangers, whether in our sleep lab or elsewhere that I've witnessed her almost total disregard for human life. But that was not with the President. It was curious and puzzling to me.

"Alright," the President replied. "I doubt I have to caution you to be aware of the mood building out there."

"I hear their expressions of anger and doubt," Finality acknowledged. "Actually, I'm surprised it hasn't happened before now. Possibly this location has a larger percentage of survivors who came from the Washington, D.C. area. Their sense of entitlement and right to know is probably a notch higher than that of the audiences we've spoken to before now.

"I'll try speaking to them from the microphone, but if that doesn't work, then I'll have to resort to a different approach."

"Might I caution you to be careful?" President Franklin added.

It was a remark that astounded me. Careful!!! She and her fiendish lackeys haven't the slightest need or idea what being careful means!! They are the Final Solution, if you will. They don't bow to anyone's shouts or armies. The fact they have "disappeared", as she likes to euphemistically phrase their onslaught, over 99% of our nation's population and are now ingesting the rest of the world's, indicates there is no limit to their capabilities or any need to be cautious.

In fact, Tom and I did a little math after the first two days of our eight presentations and roughly determined that we estimated the audiences to contain somewhere in the neighborhood of 60,000 people in each one. We simply consulted with our uniformed companions as to what they thought were the dimensions of the enclosed area in front of each speaker's platform, then estimated density of people standing within a ten square foot area and did the math. Remarkably, the occupied area for each audience was almost exactly the same... at least as far as any of us could estimate. And the concentration of people was identical... packed together; the outside perimeter of 'stains' saw to that.

Next, we multiplied the roughly 60,000, as an overall average, allowing for a few thousand, more or less, here and there, and came up with the figure of there being only about three million survivors left within the fifty States of the Union. It was a staggering figure. In just a few days time, ninety-nine percent of America's population had been taken! Where was the "care" in all that? It angered me to the point I wanted to scream out at President Franklin, "ARE YOU UTTERLY MAD?!!!" But this was not the place or time to call attention to myself. Finality was about to take center stage.

In fact, counter to all official protocol, she led the way out of Air Force One. The President, Honor Guard and then the three of us followed. I, as was customary, exited the doorway last. We filed over, up and around the front of the stage, as was the normal routine, except that this time Finality approached the lectern first. The crowd was becoming increasingly vocal as she did. The shouting was becoming constant and universal. Then Finality spoke.

"May I have your attention, please?" she said almost in a whisper.

Nothing happened.

Again she spoke, this time with a little more emphasis and volume, "I need to request that you give us your undivided attention."

No lessening of the volume or change in the audience's response followed.

Once more she calmly asked for the audience to cooperate and calm themselves. And now, there was an even louder response to her efforts. It was all-too-evident that no one in the audience had any idea who was addressing them. That was all about to change.

In what I had become uncomfortably used to witnessing over the last week or so, my sleep laboratory visitor within the time it takes to clear your throat, blink or sneeze, had disappeared from the stage and was now standing in front of our Honor Guard, in a space just wide enough to allow her now immense bulk to stand without crushing someone. She had transformed herself into the form that she normally did when Tom and I spoke. But this time she spoke. Or better described, she shouted back at the assembly that I had to think was planning on eventually taking control of the situation. In an instant those fantasies were dashed.

"ENOUGH!!" the immense, large-eyed, shapeless replicant of her associates surrounding this growing mob shouted, in a voice so loud, so thundering, so awesome in its power and force that within seconds everyone in the audience bowed their heads. Some slumped, others would have fainted and fallen, but there was not the room to do so, with everyone packed so tightly together. It was as if everyone's most horrifying dream had just taken life and stood at the foot of their bed. For the rest of our time in Richmond, there was not one word or sound coming from this audience.

And in an equally short instant, Finality transformed herself back into her disturbingly lovely disguise and motioned President Franklin to introduce us for the rest of our presentations.

Interestingly, when we made our usual Air Force One bypass salute over this audience, there was not the overt response of solidarity of waving and apparent shouting from the audience. Instead, the upturned heads and bodies were motionless. I could only assume they were still shocked and numbed by Finality's transformation and rebuke. I only hoped they had listened carefully to what we had instructed them to do and why. This was not the time for heroics. Not yet anyway.

Then on the seventh day of our cross-country trip, the next notable event occurred. Up until that time, when we started having only three stopovers per day on May 20th, I began to observe something quite intriguing taking place with Finality and the other four women that were most commonly seen around the President. There were a few others scattered among the flight and ground crew, but they kept to themselves for the most part. The honor guard spent a lot of their free time with Tom and I; it was a natural gravitation. Tom was in the Marines, and I did a hitch in the Army. The eight of them and the two of us over the course of this first week and the ones that followed became unquestionably close to one another. Just as did the

President, Finality, Colleen, President Franklin's personal secretary, Margaret or Maggie as the President most often hailed her, and Pauline or 'the Voice' as all of us called her (she and the pilot, Colonel Stan Cruz, being the only two, besides the President, authorized to announce anything over Air Force One's PA system); and Jasmine, or Jazz, the other communication specialist.

Later, I will speak more about the flight crew and the four cooks/housekeepers and maintenance personnel. Their roles in the outcome of our desperately trying to combat this invasion became pivotal. If you've ever noticed, that is so often the case. The people in the background, "the invisible ones", so often provide the steely resolve and foundation for what will later become the key to how a problem is solved or in our case how the world is saved. God bless them everyone. Give me the unsung every time. In their midst lies the promise and future of any society.

But as I was saying, Finality by the 6th or 7th day of our flights was definitely undergoing a noticeable transformation. What I sensed was a slight change before was obvious by then, at least to me who had been with her the most since this nightmare began.

I even asked Colleen about this time if I had probably mistakenly heard unfamiliar laughter coming from one of their late night social gatherings. And she off-handedly replied that it probably was coming from Finality. What really amazed me was how casually she told me this.

"Laughter!!" I exclaimed. "Coming from the 'Director-in-Chief' of Extermination Incorporated?"

"Yes," Colleen continued. "You probably don't get to see that side of her often, but we certainly do; especially more so over the last day or so. She has become quite social... even likable."

It was in response to her remark that I remembered why I felt absolutely lost and bewildered in the company of any group of women. There is a dynamic mystery that emanates from these groups that probably will still be unfathomable to any outsider such as me long after what comprises the Black Holes of the Universe is discovered and fully explained. It has to have an energy source equally as powerful as what created the Big Bang. I was completely speechless when Colleen told me this.

And I might add at this point that Colleen herself was becoming quite the confidant of President Franklin. Her expertise in things medical had impressed the President, as did her ever-present calmness and willingness to listen and offer timely and actionable advice when asked for her viewpoint. From all I could gather, the Group of Six, as I came to call them around Tom, was becoming a highly functional and supportive network. And in the midst of this unfathomable tragedy, one without any visible hope of not becoming totally devastating to all human life, that was a good omen. Finality was being drawn into something totally new to her or "it", as I preferred to refer to her out of earshot.

It was 7 a.m. on that seventh day that Air Force One made its landing approach to Robert Gray Army Airfield outside Killeen, Texas. And looking out the window I could see by far the largest assembly of citizens of anywhere we had been thus far. Throughout the eastern seaboard, Midwest and South the crowds had been consistently been in the forty-to-sixty thousand range. But here in Texas there must have been well over 100,000! It was staggering to see so many! And adding to the impact of what I was seeing was the number of military uniforms that bordered the side of the

161

crowd that would be facing Air Force One and our elevated platform.

What I have not told you yet is that we selected as many of the military reservation airfields as we could that were somewhat centrally located in a particular state. The thinking of both President Franklin and Finality was that landing there would have the greatest likelihood of providing the greatest protection and safety for everyone… both in the crowd and on Air Force One. Fort Hood, Texas was one of the largest military complexes we flew in to over the two weeks. And if the need arose, it had the most military personnel present to protect us of any of the installations that we landed in.

All in all, after we landed on the airport's single runway (it being 10,000 feet in length and easily accommodated our landing) and taxied to a stop, Air Force One's Presidential Door opened to allow our procession to file out. The tens of thousands waiting for us were as quiet as those we first encountered in Bangor. The last thing any of us thought, as we reviewed what happened later, was that anything unexpected might be about to happen. And as usual, President Franklin led us over to the stage.

Adding to our sense of business as usual, despite the grotesque reason for our having to address anyone like this, much less those gathered from over the State of Texas, was that the audience remained silent throughout all of our presentations. It was only after President Franklin finished her final statement and we were about to rise and walk off the stage that the yelling and shoving started. And in a matter of what seemed to be only seconds, a riot ensued.

We began to be pelted with wads of paper, cardboard, then larger and more lethal items like rocks and bottles. And the guttural sounds of anger only grew in intensity. I never knew whether it was directed at Finality, who by this time had resumed her now-most-common appearance as the matron of malice who I first met on our flight to Washington, D.C. But soon enough it was certainly clear that it was all of us who were under attack.

Our honor guard was just able to maneuver round the edge of the stage and worm their way between the soldiers stationed at Fort Hood who were providing the desperate line of defense between us and the audible and visible mob. The two of our uniformed service people who were armed waited until we got down the platform steps to chamber live rounds into their rifles and turned to face the audience, which was by now beginning to surge forward, dangerously pressing the leading edge of Fort Hood's vestiges of surviving personnel against the military personnel. Our cordon of protection was about to break, if for no other reason than just the weight of humanity pressing forward. Then shots were fired into the air... by whom I was never sure. I didn't believe it was from our two security guards. Their orders were not to fire warning shots, should it become necessary to use them. I had to assume it was from those providing us what was by then a meager zone of safety.

It was just at this point, one in which everyone begins to mutter small incantations, whimper, call out to their deity of choice or beg for mercy that another of those unforgettable transformations occurred.

Finality, apparently through her seemingly endless supply of manifestations and orchestrations to direct and control her shroud-covered alien invaders, instantaneously signaled to them in some way and brought thousands of her compatriots immediately surging around and through us to backup the Fort Hood soldiers. It was like a flash flood of blackness. They were upon us in an instant. They were soundless and you could not see the person who was standing next to you a second before. The suddenness of it sucked the air from around us, making it difficult to breathe… much less comprehend what was happening.

And apparently within that same couple of seconds, Finality appeared back onto the then empty stage and assumed her towering presence again. But this time, there was no scanning of the mob rushing toward us.

"YOU HAVE LESS THAN ONE SECOND TO STOP AND CEASE THIS OUTRAGE!!" she bellowed, in volume that was as clear as the crackling of thunder at dusk and so loud that if anyone was able and alive to hear miles from our present location they would have understood every word. "STOP NOW OR THOSE IN THE FRONT WILL BEGIN TO DISAPPEAR… IMMEDIATELY."

But they didn't stop, and many did disappear. But not just in the front but scattered throughout the rioting throng. It wasn't something that any of the other passengers aboard Air Force One would have been aware of; I only learned later in conversations with Finality. In those frantic moments we were too terrified and were dashing headlong back to the entrance of the plane. Its metal outline appeared to offer us some hope for survival. But had that mob reached it, I had no doubt they would have destroyed it along with all of us inside.

But within a matter of a few more seconds after Finality's ultimatum, bringing in her reserve forces that now surged ahead of Fort Hood's troops, which now made a tight circle of "stains" completely encircling the once placid audience and the disappearance of hundreds of those in that audience, they were brought literally to their knees. And that was the position that Finality stated they had to assume immediately as well. The near riot was quelled, but at the needless expense of more people. It made each of us sick who boarded the plane. We were here to preserve life, not to prompt a massacre.

And because of this reaction and resulting tragedy, it caused us to modify our future presentations that day and each one thereafter. From that point on during President Franklin's introduction, she both reassured and cautioned each audience that they had to listen, perform what was to be asked of them, and stay in place until we left. It was for everyone's protection. And to back that up, Finality thereafter had the "stains" come forward from the outlying perimeter to supplement any protection personnel in front of each audience. As distasteful as their nearby presence was, at least it would allow us to safely bring our message to everyone and heighten everyone's chances of ultimate survival. But we never got over the loss of those needless deaths in Texas.

It was on Day 9 of our presentations that the third rather significant event occurred. Leading up to that point there were certainly signs of its presence. And at this point I probably should make one brief comment. While I know that anyone reading this might have a sincere desire to know all that is possible about the people who were on board Air Force One; the truth is, that is really not germane to what I am attempting to document in my retelling what occurred over this particular month as well as what led up to such a senseless and bewildering tragedy. However, to the best of my ability to analyze human, and most outrageous of all, extraterrestrial characteristics and changes in behavior, I should at least try to make an exception in a few cases. And the first one is the most challenging: Finality.

She (or, "it", as I prefer to address her when not in her presence) continued on the path that I began to notice some days before this. And the most significant aspect of that was her appearing to steadily lose stamina and the ability to concentrate. It was like she had some neurological disease that was weakening her and seemed to be accelerating its effects by the day. I noticed more pauses in her speech, less quickness in her movements and gestures and probably most oddly of all, more willingness to listen and engage in conversation rather than just issue orders. And she slept more and longer. She gave me the sense that she was almost becoming vulnerable.

The exception being when she was alone with me. Then it was like she had to portray herself as being totally in control of any situation... and me. It was like I was someone that she had to have absolute authority over; almost as if there was some lurking fear of me, as ridiculous as that must sound.

Tom, on the other hand, was even tempered and had his "game face on" every waking moment. That's what I really liked about him. He may not have been the leader of nations, but he was the bedrock that allowed them to conduct their business. And he knew if they were not doing it with enough dedication. He had a sense about him. He could almost smell fraud or purposeful error. And he knew accomplished work. He could complement you sincerely or redirect you with equal energy if you were becoming careless or detached. And most of all for this journey into the very heart of the unknown, he was a masterful musician. He could tune any instrument to play at its peak, and then he could turn around and play it. But he couldn't sing worth a square nickel. He above everyone else, including his wife Colleen who did manage to keep all twenty-four of Air Force One's occupants alive and functioning throughout this period, kept us as upbeat and focused as was possible.

Without the two of them this mission would have been doomed. Depression, doubt and denial would have ended our attempts to stall this invasion long before we had finished our flights.

President Franklin, on the other hand, began to appear more distracted, almost overwhelmed by it all. And who wouldn't be. There is no list of Presidential candidate prerequisites that specifies that to be a qualified individual to hold this office one should be able to combat and triumph over an alien invasion. In my mind she had performed superbly from that first day in the Oval Office until the 8th day of our cross-country mission. But on the morning of our 9th day she appeared completely overwhelmed or possibly sick with some virus. I asked Colleen to check her out and don't let her pull any "I'm the President" excuses for avoiding rest or taking any medications. We needed her well. And failing that, at least mobile and present. To show up at any of these rendezvous sites on Air Force One without the President on board and visible, whether she speaks or not, would be disastrous. No one would believe us. It would convince anyone that the takeover was complete and everyone was doomed.

The President's lethargy, as worrisome as it was, had to be evaluated by Colleen, our medical person, and at least make it possible for her to walk out of Air Force One and up onto the stage and sit through what the others of us had to say; otherwise, our mission was doomed. Better still, she should hopefully be able to walk to the microphone one time and express her gratitude for the bravery of each person there and introduce Finality. We could then sit her directly behind the lectern and two of us sitting beside could keep her propped upright through the presentation.

So just after our flight took off from Springfield,

Illinois, for the short hop to the Indianapolis International Airport, I cornered Colleen and asked to check out both Finality and President Franklin. And at that time I noticed that even Colleen didn't look too well herself. She admitted she was running a slight temperature and thought maybe she was getting the flu. And with all the time these three spent together, it made sense to me that maybe each of them had contracted the same virus.

Quickly, she ran back to the onboard clinic and got some fever suppression, antiviral and pain management medications for everyone; along with those she even took some antidepressants to issue to herself and to the President and Finality. By the time we exited the plane, after some delay waiting for the meds to have their desired effect; we managed to complete this presentation and the next one later that afternoon in Lansing, Michigan without too much variation from our usual routine. I did notice, however, that Finality did not project quite as tall a figure when I did my presentation. And I sense she was weaving back and forth a bit. I can't imagine what would have happened if she fell over. It would have been like a four story, water-filled balloon hitting the ground? But somehow I doubted it would come to that. Even aliens have to keep up appearances.

Fortunately, we were able to forge on despite the emerging illness in some of our crew and the changes in motivation, even personality, in those who were falling ill. Who could be shocked by anyone getting sick or having these emotional reactions? I was frankly amazed by the day that somehow we were able to keep on performing as well as we did and continue to meet the almost impossibly demanding schedule. And what surprised me even more was that increasingly I was having to bring discussions and arguments back into focus and make the necessary summations for us to resolve problems and find solutions. Even Finality was increasingly taking a more minor role in these conversations. It was one of the first signs that I recognized to her becoming frailer. And, despite my dearest wish that she could disappear herself... like countless others had in recent weeks because of her and her associates demonic appetites, we all needed her. She was part of the "temporary stay or solution" we were presenting at these airports. Without her right now, all of us would be consumed in a matter of weeks. But as I have already alluded to, she studiously maintained herself in a stoic and in-control façade when alone with me. My sanity seemed to be stretching and loosening like a strangely supple rubber band. But for how much longer could any of us continue?

And the breaking point began to show in each of us on May 25th, our 11th day on board Air Force One. We had slept in that morning due to our having a very short distance to fly this day to the three designated airports, and our last airport for the 24th was in Bismarck, North Dakota. It was 8:30 a.m. when Air Force One taxied over to the speaker's platform and came to a complete halt for our first presentation of the day. We were never able to hear anything going on outside the plane until the engines were shut off and one of its doors was swung open. And up until this point, as I have described previously, there were only rare exceptions when we heard anything from the audiences. And never had we heard anything from the untold number of "stains" that surrounded the survivors at the previous airports. But that all changed when we assembled at the doorway and began to file down the stairs onto the tarmac.

Greeting us was an angry sounding murmer; it was like nothing I had ever heard before. It sounded like thousands upon thousands of wild beasts who had not eaten in days and were starving, but in addition they were cornered by larger prey and would now have to fight for their lives to secure needed nourishment. It was both a desperate, building roar and a menacing one. It signaled that death was inevitable for either the hunter or the hunted.

I turned to Tom who was behind me and asked, "What is that sound? Are we about to experience another audience's frustration and have a mad rush toward us before we even get off the plane?"

"I certainly hope not," Tom answered. "Just the same, it seems to be a more ominous sound, more in concert rather than just scattered shouts or noise. It seems to resemble something like a guttural growling, expressing a rage over a denied right or appetite."

"Hmm," I answered, becoming more worried by the second, "maybe you're onto something there. It almost sounds like my stomach when I haven't eaten in a day or so, but with it being broadcasted and magnified thousands of times over. Do you think this audience is starving and just too weak to express it any other way, other than in a groan-like growl?

Tom quickly replied, "Or should we consider it might be the 'stains' expressing something. After all, we've never heard one of them speak. We don't even know if they do. Maybe this is their only means of verbalization. And maybe, just maybe, it's them who are hungry…"

"I'm going to catch up with Finality and ask her," I hurriedly answered. "The state she is in lately, she may not even be able to hear them. If you are right and if it is their manner of expressing displeasure or, much worse… anger, we and everyone else here are desperately vulnerable."

Worming my way back through the Honor Guard, I

spied Finality still sitting in a leather-bound armchair in the conference room. She had not yet made any attempt to join the party about to exit the plane. And that, in itself, was curious.

"Finality," I called out as I rushed into the room, "Are you hearing what is going on outside right now? Tom and I are worried that it may signal another serious response from the audience or worse."

"What do you mean by 'or worse'?" she snapped. This, of course, was her usual way of responding to my questions or comments. Our relationship from that first meeting in the laboratory never changed. It was as if she knew I saw deeper inside her than anyone else aboard the plane. It was almost as if she was defensive; the reason for which I would never be able to grasp. What in heaven's name did I have or possess that might cause that kind of reaction in an ever-aware and keenly deadly alien?

"Come on, Finality," I answered, now equally curt and defensive. "All of us are doing exactly as you demanded we do. Why do you have to be so belligerent towards me when I ask a simple question? We are simply worried and wanted to know if you are aware of anything about to happen amongst your fellow-beings. Tom and I are concerned that it might be them who are trying to express something that only you might understand. We don't want to walk into some trap or precipitate some disaster for these folks waiting outside to hear what we have to say. Please… help us understand what is going on?"

"Alright," she conceded. "I was a little tired yet, and was trying to catch a last minute pause in our daily routine. Allow me to get by you, and I will go to the doorway and try to figure out what you are hearing or seeing."

Once she did weave her way through the waiting Honor Guard, and those of us who are the usual speakers each day, she came to the open doorway and listened. She remained immobile for at least two or three minutes, seemingly just listening and cocking her head side-to-side, as if trying to catch odd bits of information. Finally, she turned to us waiting to exit the plane and spoke.

"There is a problem, and it is a major one at that," she began. "It seems what I am hearing my cohorts express is impatience and disgust with my leadership. They are famished and are undeterred in wanting to begin the final assault. In short, there is an open revolt at play here; something I have never encountered before. Of course, I have never taken the pains I have with you and these flights to stall an invasion of a collapsing world. I don't expect them to understand my motivation, especially when I am unable to fully understand it myself. And believe me, it is exhausting for me. As you may have noticed, I am steadily losing strength and the will to continue as we are.

"And complicating matters further, there is no armed militia here. Instead, there are a very few local and state troopers. They are pitifully powerless to stop my associates should they embark on an all-out assault. And we only have the two military guards on board to protect you. That is woefully inadequate.

"Each of you will have to stay inside here while I venture out and begin a process that I've never had to undertake before. After this, I will never be able to accompany them again. And the only salvation you have is that they are incapable of communicating with their compatriots located at the remaining airports or at the ones we have already been to. Stay inside here, whatever else you do. And close and secure this door behind me. Alert the flight crew to restart the engines if I fail. You will then have to proceed without me."

And before anyone could question or object, she essentially disappeared from sight. What followed is only a glimpse of what I viewed outside one of Air Force One's port windows. And even with the outside door secured and the onboard circulating air system at full capacity, I could hear a frightful roaring. And the air outside had turned black as with the swirling of tens of thousands of "stains" and Finality, probably assuming her immense form for direct combat. It appeared that reasoning was not her first choice of reconciling their anger and frustration. Like everywhere, violent beings appear to only understand and respond to violence.

At one point the huge frame of our plane shook violently from what must have been passing wind gusts from the surging back and forth of the combatants. And as I looked closely, when enough light broke through that I could see them, I observed the audience, one of the smallest we would address, lying flat on the ground with their hands covering their heads.

The awesome battle lasted at least ten minutes, with total blackness surging back and forth across my window. And then as quickly as it began, it was silent and there was full daylight. Looking downward at the end of our exit ramp I could then see Finality standing there, motioning for me to come out. But fearful that I somehow had misunderstood her, I requested that the others wait until I opened the doorway and double-checked that I was interpreting her hand gestures correctly.

And when I did, I heard her yell out, "Come on out Connor, and bring everyone with you. The issue has been resolved."

It being "resolved" would not have been the word or phrase that I would have chosen. Maybe "overpowered", "beaten back" or "vanquished" would have better described what I heard and saw. But I knew better at that very moment not to challenge Finality in any way. If there was any blood coursing through any veins in her form, it was surely flowing at peak velocity and temperature at that moment. I didn't want to get tossed somersaulting in the air by some off-handed remark. So, instead, I replied, "Ok".

She did not fill us in with what took place; at least not until a few days later when she and I had what had to be one of the most pivotal conversations in the course of human pre or current history. The President and Finality reassured the South Dakotans that their safety was secure for the foreseeable future or more specifically for the next two weeks. And our presentation went on as usual, as it did the next three days.

Thus, this ended the first four incidents that I wanted to brief you on. The fifth and most earth-changing one began on our fifteen day, as we were leaving our presentation in Alaska and heading for Hawaii. Those next three hours were ones that would initiate the world never being the same thereafter. It involved the permanent solution for our salvation.

SIXTEEN: FINALITY'S ULTIMATUM

Don't let my jumping from one incident to another give you the impression that there were not significant developments both on the ground and inside Air Force One during these two weeks. There were.

For starters there were the ongoing emotional and health changes within our in-flight personnel. President Franklin continued her steady decline in resiliency and withdrew more and more. It was as if this entire tragedy was somehow happening due to some failure on her part. She was internalizing a cosmic drama that was far beyond any human's ability to anticipate or comprehend. But telling her this did little to ease her approaching a catatonic state at times. It was only after I met privately with her just before our flight from Hawaii to California ended that she began to gain some measure of balance and restoration of her self-confidence.

Then there was Colleen. She, without question, became the "doctor" to us all. All the personnel on Air Force One came to her on a regular basis for counseling or for some kind of balm to ease real or imaginary pains or aches. She spent three-quarters of her time in the small, onboard clinic. The only time Tom and she were together was for an occasional meal and at night. Otherwise, she was our healer-in-chief.

Tom, on the other hand, stayed his unflappable self. When my insides were quivering, and I sensed that I was going to be tongue-tied at the next stopover, he could prod me with some tale or joke or supervisory goad… like he did countless times with me in our sleep lab; and I would forge ahead. Without Colleen and him any success our flights had would have been doubtful. Finality knew what she was doing when she commanded them to travel with us from Palm Springs.

Just the same, Finality by the time we arrived at Elmendorf Air Force Base in Anchorage, Alaska, had the appearance of someone who had aged fifty years from the first time I saw her on the flight to Washington, D.C. She spoke in an almost whisper. And there was a glaze beginning to cover both of her eyes… like cataracts. What had appeared to me initially as possible fatigue now was clearly an apparent unstoppable aging process; likely brought about by her decision to assume a human body rather than remain in her "stain" one. At this point I began to think that possibly she was sacrificing herself to gain our lasting protection. But I still couldn't be sure.

Lest I forget, there were the honor guards and general cabin crew. They were the professions, who kept our mission literally on course and nourished. I never heard any complaints or griping from any of them. They represented the best tradition of our service personnel. And it makes me so happy to say that they, to an individual, have rejoined us where I am presently writing this account.

Finally, there were the crowds of people at the airports. During our final days we couldn't help but observe there appeared to be some signs of hunger and the disturbing effects of overcrowding. But there was always a steely patience. People everywhere wanted desperately to know what we had to say, and they exhibited remarkable hope for a future. Even up to the time we flew off from Alaska, each and every audience always, aside from the one in Texas, would lift their arms and wave and shout at us as Air Force One wagged her wings when we flew so low over them we could pick out individual faces. The sound of her engines, the sight of her majestic outline and what she represented as a symbol of our nation's will to survive must have invigorated them. And I certainly hoped they followed our advice after we left. But we had no way of actually knowing this. There was no communication between any of the airfields we visited or between our plane and them. Our country and everyone on our planet were totally isolated from one another.

But now I must spend the necessary time with what Finality said to me in those hours we flew from Alaska to Hawaii. And to do so, I will start at the beginning of her conversation that mid-morning after we take off.

"Before I go into any detail about what role you'll play in your final presentation in California," she began, "the one which will describe what has to be done to insure a permanent reprieve from my associates and my relentless quest of your world, I need to fill you in on critical details about the origins of your humanity and later where and how your civilization and immunity from our invasion long before this one might have occurred. While you and the other members of this life-saving assignment were either sleeping or attempting to get some sort of rest, I left you, even if my exterior form was still present. Over these last two weeks I have scoured this world for detailed information about your world in an attempt to discover some solution to prevent me and my kind from annihilating the remainder of you."

"Have you found it?" I asked impulsively, knowing I was interrupting her train of thought, but eager to hear if she was going to give me the answer we were all waiting and hoping for.

"No. Not yet. Or at least I hope not yet. But I must warn you that, as you have no doubt noticed, my strength is waning fast. I may touch on the reason why that is later, but for now, I must continue with my original train of thought. From outlining all this with you, I am hopeful an answer may present itself. I have tried and tried to discover it."

"You mean even you have no idea what might permanently save us?" I cried out, which drew an immediate gesture from her to silence me. "How am I supposed to help? Have you forgotten? I am just a guy you stumbled upon in a one-of-a-thousand sleep laboratories, scattered across our nation and world."

"In that regard, you are quite wrong," she cautioned. "Even though I had no firm intention to attempt to save some remnant of your civilization, seeking you out was not happenstance. Before we invade a world, I do a fairly detailed survey of it and its inhabitants. And as I have already discussed with you, what brings me in the first place is the wafting scent of a dying world. I can pick it up thousands of light years from its origin.

"And in the process of exploring your world, I came to realize there were isolated pockets of goodness, even godliness, amongst you. But two questions had to be answered and then pivotal decisions had to be made. Would I find someone with the temporary immunity from our attack and would that same individual have the fighting spirit and potential for helping me save this world? And how would I go about organizing a team for accomplishing this? Once I discovered you, I was able to work out a plan. I had already arrived at all this by the time I revealed myself to you.

"Saying that, I must implore you to pay the closest attention possible to what I am about to discuss with you. Forget about any preconceived opinions you have about me or yourself. Let your mind envelope what I say. Forget about who or what I am and what has already happened to your people. You must concentrate. Time is running out. Listen carefully to me!

"Now I must continue where I left off. And brushing aside the issue of how mankind came to have essentially your present appearance and capacity to learn and innovate, I need rather to begin with who and where humanity's actual migration began and the major signposts along the way. From that review, may then develop the solution for your ultimate means of survival. And this will undoubtedly be my final, extended conversation with you. Included in it will obviously be some comments of how I view you, the manner in which you've handled these last weeks since our initial meeting, and what I perceive lies ahead for you and your race. In short, all of you were too easily underestimated by me. I made a mistake bringing my legions here. But it may too late.

"So let me begin, roughly 60,000 years ago, in a region of southwest Africa...in the arid bush country or more precisely, the desert region of what is now Namibia. It is a country just north of South Africa and has the Atlantic Ocean defining its western border. It was here a uniquely skilled and adventurous people began a steady migration to and through the northeast portions of Africa.

"Within a relatively short period of time, following the shorelines of Africa, the Arabian Peninsula, around the Middle Eastern countries of what are now Iraq, Iran and Pakistan down around India and the countries above Indonesia, they eventually were able to sail from there to the landmass of Australia. It is there they first settled, about 50,000 years ago. It was these remarkable ancestors of yours that made the first successful attempt to establish permanent settlements beyond Africa's boundaries. And the peoples there eventually became known as Aborigines. From all indications this far-reaching, eastern migration involved about ten percent of these original, migratory adventurers. The other ninety percent of them eventually veered northward, once they reached the Arabian Peninsula.

"It needs to be emphasized at this point that these migrations involved peoples who were hunters/gatherers. There was no agriculture, no permanent settlements, nor organized governmental entities. They were composed of individual family groups and were essentially tribal. It was a precarious existence, only being fortified by its members' loyalty and dedication to their individual band's survival. But throughout this period of prehistory, there was something of great importance brewing. They were thinking, analyzing and most important of all, feeling beings. No one can underestimate the importance of that latter attribute. As much as intelligence and innovation is valued in all cultures, it is the heartfelt feelings of humanity that drove its most remarkable advances. They were neither stupid nor aimless wanderers.

"Two events then occurred some millennia later that should capture our attention and possibly lead us to our solution and give you some direction for what you and your associates may do if we are somehow successful in finding an answer.

"The first was that these Asian nomads reached the edge of what is now the present day coastline of eastern Siberia. And the driving urge to move beyond there drove them to cross the Aleutian land bridge separating that region from the Americas. It was, after all, the middle of your last Ice Age. (*See Appendix: Last Glacial Maximum Map*) Then again, these same intrepid voyagers sailed in view of or walked along any exposed shorelines, which now border Alaska, Canada and Washington State. By the time they reached Oregon's border the ice shelf was diminishing rapidly in height and volume. But there were still the impenetrable forests and rushing rivers with their high cliffs along its coastline to greet them. For their ultimate long-term survival, they knew they had to venture further into this land's interior. But how and where?

"The answer came when they discovered the outflow into the Pacific Ocean of what is now called the Umpqua River. It was a relatively slow, meandering river… at least compared to the others in that coastal region. They then followed up its length to its source, high in the Cascade Mountains. And from there it was a relatively easy march down into the high desert region of south-central Oregon. I presume they must have trekked down and round what is now called 'Fort Rock' and into the Summer Lake Region. Ultimately, they settled north of what is now the small community of Paisley, Oregon. And the date for this settlement was 14,300 years ago. It was the America's first settlement. (*See APPENDIX: Paisley, Oregon Map*)

"The other marker that I believe has particular significance for our primary mission of finding a permanent survival solution for you and the others of your world happened in what is now identified as southeastern Turkey, to south of which is the Syrian border. Further on in that general direction would eventually comprise Mesopotamia and the Fertile Crescent. It was here, within a relatively easy walking distance for those early nomads and hunter/gatherers that human civilization arose.

"Something stunning and of utmost significance predated this hallmark event. Humanity had been struggling for countless eons to simply survive in small bands, wandering from place to place to find adequate shelter and enough food. Their almost aimless wandering had allowed them the opportunity to see lands across your globe, but nothing as yet had given them lasting protection.

"And I might add that the slight scent of death began to eek forth from this world. It was about this time that your planet caught my attention. But then, in almost an instant, these come-hither odors were gone. Something happened. And I sense that maybe the secret of your lasting protection has something to do with what occurred in this region of Turkey. I am hoping you and I can come to some conclusion as to what it was during this all-important conversation. Time is running out for you… and for me. The hordes will be unleashed for their final assault if we don't."

"What event or discovery did you find that is so important?" I exclaimed.

"In this area in what is now the country of Turkey is located a hilltop, archeological site known as Göbekli Tepe. It is about 9 miles northeast of Urfa. (*See APPENDIX : Map Site of Göbekli Tepe*). Uncovered after thousands of years of accumulated wind-blown soil were stunning T-shaped columns of various sizes and heights. They were assembled in circles of various sizes. And etched on them were an amazing assortment of animals, insects, spiders and birds. (*See APPENDIX: Pillars at Göbekli Tepe Representing Outstretched Arms and Pillars at Göbekli Tepe with Image of Vultures*). Most remarkable of all, scientists have been able to date this site as being constructed 11,500 years ago. It is by far the oldest structure of its kind ever constructed by those earliest hunter/gatherers who left southern Africa 60,000 years ago.

"And it is no accident that the first signs of agriculture and organized communities and cities began in the region nearby. Something so basic and fundamental was occurring at that site; something that would alter the direction and potential survival of your species. Before its construction, your kind was attracting our attention. Then, as quickly as I was becoming aware of it, your accelerating worth or value and potential consumptive presence for us vanished. We moved on. Why was that, I now have to ask you? What happened there that caused us to divert our attention elsewhere until recently? Why did we ignore you in those earlier times and then return when we could not help but notice the odor of carrion... of decay?

"To answer this question is the main reason why I chose you to first reveal myself and then force you to come along with me on this trip. While it's true you did possess the temporary answer to postpone your world's total annihilation, it was the answer to this historical puzzle that ultimately led me to choose you to be here at this moment.

"Certainly, I was hoping I would be in better shape to assist you in answering this riddle, but I'm not. My strength is dwindling faster each day, as you may have noticed. Unfortunately, you only have the remainder of this day to come up with what you think is the answer to my questions. I will have Tom perform your portion of the presentation once we arrive in Hawaii, but by the time we reach California tonight, you must have the answers to my questions. Whatever it was that allowed those earliest humans to avoid our sweeping in upon them, like we have now, has to be uncovered and then initiated tonight! I can no longer protect you or anyone else on this plane or on the ground below us. I won't even be able to speak before the audience in California. It will be your sole responsibility to do so. All I will be able to manage is to assume my altered form and peer down over you and the audience. And the only way you'll know if you have found the answer is when I have disappeared, along with all my associates. If you haven't, the consumption will resume and all of you will disappear within seconds of your coming up to speak at that lectern and having nothing new to report to them."

SEVENTEEN: THE FIFTH AND FINAL INCIDENT

I let out an audible gasp at her command and frantically moaned, "Why me?   Why choose me to be responsible for attempting to save humanity?   Is this some kind of sick trick; your final act of toying with us?   I have no qualifications for answering such questions... or any questions for that matter.   Ask the President.   Ask Colleen.   Tom.   Ask the audience in Hawaii.   But not me... for heaven's sake and for the sake of all who eagerly await the answer of what has to be done to preserve life on this world."

"No, it is you who must answer my questions," her voice rising in response and with an air of impatience.   "And you are wasting valuable time protesting.   I am going to leave you now.   Spend the next twelve hours contemplating what has happened, what I have told you and what must be done.   No one will bother you in here.   And you are not to consult with anyone.   It is only in absolute solitude that your mind and heart will possibly arrive at the answers to my questions and reach the conclusion necessary for your safety and well being.   And I might add, before I leave you and most likely never speak with you again, you might also try some praying.   I can imagine that it has probably been a long time since you have, but it might help as well. From my investigations, it does appear to at least give others some comfort and peace of mind… both of which you're going to need before you can find the necessary inspiration and answers."

And as she said that, she rose slowly and what almost appeared painfully, and left me alone in the Conference Room. I had never felt so alone before or since. The drone of the airplane's engines echoed in my head. All the sounds, whether it was the air circulating, crew walking up and down the outside hallway or the pounding of my own heart, each began to magnify and become more intense and distracting. I was beginning to panic.

Within seconds of her leaving, the Conference Room became too crowded and too small… even though I was the only one in there. I had to escape it and this airplane.

Years ago, I became claustrophobic after attempting to rescue a woman injured from a car accident. She had run off the road and totally demolished her car which was impaled into and around a huge Douglas fir tree, located about fifty feet off the roadway.

I must have spent an hour extricating and then attempting to resuscitate her. Covered in blood I eventually went back to my car and hurried to meet my family for a reunion at a lodge, near the Oregon Caves. It was to be a joyous occasion, and it was to begin by our taking a tour of the caves themselves. This tour would then be followed by a luncheon and a night's stay at the lodge.

I hurriedly tried to wash myself and got another set of clothes I brought along with me once I got to the Lodge. Remarkably, I was then able to warmly greet everyone at the Cave's entrance, just as had been our prearranged plan; all seemed back to normal… until I entered the cave.

Immediately, I found myself struggling to breath and

terrified to have others so close around me in that enclosed space. I had in the course of my attempted rescue earlier that day become severely claustrophobic. And for several years afterward I could not use elevators or be in overcrowded, darkened rooms without having the same reaction. Gradually, this condition subsided... until the moment I was alone in Air Force One's Conference Room.

In hopes of relieving the progressively worsening tightness in my chest and shortness of breath, I ran around the oval table and seized the doorknob and attempted to turn it and pull the only door into the room open. I was shocked to find it was locked! Finality had somehow done so to ensure that I stayed inside and alone.

I began to pace frantically around the small room, and then on impulse dropped down onto the floor, crawling under the oval table. Huddled there in an attempt to gain a measure of control back, I eventually pushed aside a couple of chairs and pulled my knees up to my chest. Closing my eyes tightly, I began to rock and hum. It was precisely the actions of someone undergoing a massive psychotic breakdown.

My deepest fears, the tragedies I had witnessed over the past three weeks, the horror of meeting, listening to, enduring the presence of Finality and now having to somehow come up with an answer to what might save our planet from total annihilation of all human life had reached its peak. I felt my mind beginning to crack open and spill out all rationality, confidence and hope. How could I achieve what was being demanded of me or sustain one more minute of this nightmare?

And then the tears and wailing grief started. It was like I was attempting to mourn for all who had disappeared. My cries had to have been heard throughout the plane, but no one ever came to the door to check on me.

I became engulfed in grief. Losing my family three years ago and now the impact of these last week's overcame me. I was trapped in this room with an utterly impossible charge, from an alien who could perform acts and feats of incomprehensible madness and evil. And now she had told me to make it all better.

I probably sat rocking and moaning under that table for at least forty-five minutes to an hour. Time became meaningless. But eventually I remember myself sitting upright and silent. Out of reflex, I did something I had not done in years: I crossed myself, while repeating the words, "in the name of the Father, the Son and the Holy Ghost".

Maybe it was a prayer, a cry, a yielding or a humble request for guidance… to this day I could not say. But it wasn't long thereafter that I reached up from under the table to grab and pull down a stack of blank, bond paper along with a couple of pencils, which slid off onto the floor in front of me.

While I was sure that my claustrophobia was still lurking at the border of my subconscious mind, so long as I stayed under that table I felt a measure of security and some escape from it and from my all-consuming grief. I knew I had to at least make an attempt at finding an answer to Finality's riddle. And, totally out of character for the last three decades of my life and especially since the loss of my family, I had spontaneously summoned any heavenly hosts wandering in my vicinity to guide me.

Obviously, I wasn't at all sure where to begin in this search, but I sensed that Finality had not given me the information she did without herself thinking that there might be something associated with it that might assist me. So, I began to review in my mind what she had said and started writing random thoughts and ideas down on the blank pages in front of me. Little by little I tried to connect any possible relationship that might connect them. It was a tedious process.

And as I progressed, I began to enlist the wisdom and earnest training and guidance my professors in theology school had tried so vainly to instill in me years ago. Actually, I was attempting in those hours I was imprisoned alone, once I had somewhat recovered from my total emotional collapse, to enlist anything and everything in my life to construct a framework around which some solution could be found to present to our last audience in Sacramento, California, in about four hours.

What follows now is the framework that emerged from my initial scribbling. And later on you will have an opportunity to read the actual speech that I gave that late night , the 29th of May.

First off, I had to surmise what was so important that happened at Göbekli Tepe in what was now the country of Turkey. It had to be something basic and fundamental for Finality to mention it. What would bring nomadic people together to erect something so permanent that its remnants would last these thousands of years? It was a remarkable departure from ANYTHING ever conceived, much less built, prior to that time. If our true ancestors had begun their worldwide migration 60,000 years ago, it took them 48,500 more years to decide to do this. It signaled one of the most significant shifts in human history, if not the most significant. One major reason is that it marked the earliest known ending of prehistory. Here were foundation stones for history to begin.

Also, the prominence of animal and bird life that was carved into their upright columns intrigued me, and especially that of the vulture. That was particularly so, given that Finality, herself, described her legions as cosmic, migratory vultures. It was as if these early hunters/gatherers were uniquely aware of Finality's past vulture-like presence, but more concretely they used this creature to highlight their ritual of what I have heard it referred to as "sky burials". There were some Native American Indians who also practiced this ritual by building scaffolding and placing their deceased loved ones on it. And throughout these earliest burial rituals, vultures were prominent in these reverential ceremonies of final departure. Most importantly, through this process, it appeared to me these ancients were ceremoniously honoring their own ancestors.

And, in addition, what apparently took place at this long-ago site in Turkey had a regional significance. Bands of nomadic people assembled together to build this structure. It was a temple. It signaled a dramatic change from individual or tribal ritual to a collective, reverential response to what mattered most to them. Significantly, this change ultimately required the establishment of permanent settlements to build and maintain it. And from this step came the advent of agriculture, domesticated animals and eventually cities strung across the Fertile Crescent.

Something felt and believed so passionately led to bands of people coming together to build this first of all temples or permanent buildings. I believe its creation had to be their way of protesting death and, equally so, it was their resounding and earth-shaking attempt to affirm life.

And just about then it struck me what was the overpowering importance of this oldest of all temples, as fundamentally naive or unsophisticated as it may appear to present-day humans. It was a place of worship. And it was their desire to build and maintain it that led to those of us who followed them to become civilized. Its presence marks an earth-shaking moment in human history. Probably one not equaled until this latest one which may mark the extermination of all humanity, unless a remedy can be discovered.

It was at this point that I sensed what the permanent reprieve for all of us might be. In the time remaining I then set about preparing the message that I would deliver in less than four hours at our last destination.

EIGHTEEN: SACRAMENTO, CALIFORNIA

Truthfully, I was not aware of our landing or departure from Honolulu. So much of what I did after my total collapse in the Conference Room is now blurred. My last hours in there, before Finality came to release me just before my presentation, were filled with my composing the upcoming message. But I had no idea what might happen if I was correct in my assumption of what had to be done for all of us to be granted a permanent release from captivity. However, I certainly knew what would occur if I misjudged. We'd all disappear.

Not being of an overly religious inclination, I cannot honestly say I had any other noteworthy spiritual moments in that Conference Room, aside from the one brief prayer of supplication I muttered after my emotional collapse. Just the same, I do recall a certain mystifying calm seep into that room thereafter as I sat scribbling, marking out and rewriting ideas for my presentation, while sitting under that oval table.

When the Conference Room door opened, standing there were both President Franklin and Finality. Few words were exchanged, other than President Franklin asking me if I was ok, and my replying I wasn't sure. Ignoring my comment, Finality just gestured for me to follow them outside and up onto the large platform. Before it silently stood the largest audience we ever faced. There were to be no introductions... no other speakers.

The President just motioned for me to walk forward to the line of microphones in front of the lectern and begin. Just prior to my doing so, I did lean forward and whispered into her ear how much I admired her and appreciated her confidence in me. And then, without thinking, I said, "I think we will be ok." My saying so took both her and me by surprise. But I felt it was the least I could say, given the devastation and losses she shouldering.

Whatever she and Finality had agreed upon before that moment I was never to know. Somehow, though, given my being locked up in that Conference Room for all those soul-searching hours, it did not seem that far beyond the realm of what is natural, given the ghoulish circumstances we had been facing for almost the last month, for the President at least to have grave reservations about both my ability and the content of what I was about to say.

As calmly as was possible at that moment, I then nodded to each of them, shrugged almost imperceptibly to Tom and Colleen and walked up to the battery of microphones. Somehow, again, the airport personnel had managed to hoard a supply of diesel fuel, enough to provide lighting for Air Force One to land safely at night and to allow the immense audience in front of me to be illuminated, as well as most of our stage. Not as well lit were the tens of thousands of "stains" surrounding all of us. But you could see the black border if you squinted long enough. They were all still there, impatiently waiting for the nod from Finality or more likely for the internal release from whatever impulse drove them to perform their consumptive ritual. An air of doom, along with resolute resignation and a remarkable determination of wanting to live hung in the air by this audience before me. Clearing my throat, I began.

"What I am about to say has not been told to another individual or audience prior to your hearing it. And as you know, if it is found insufficient, neither you nor I or those seated behind me will see the light of dawn about four hours from now. For some reason, unknown to me and probably it will always remain so; I have been commanded to speak at this moment. And for the sake of some clarity, and I hope brevity, I will break this message down into two major parts. First, I need to address how we possibly managed to get ourselves in a position that led to the awful tragedy that engulfs us, and second, what can be done to permanently stop it. We will know soon enough if what is said now is sufficient to do so.

"60,000 years ago a march by some resilient members of humanity began to extend the borders of human exploration and occupation, one not unlike at least two others that occurred before this one. Among the remarkable accomplishments that this final migration achieved, which has eventually led to us being assembled here this night, were that those early hunter/gatherers ancestors were able eventually to march or sail across our entire planet, erect the first man-made monuments to signal or honor our beliefs, deepest hopes and longings and finally to initiate the advent of agriculture and domestication. It has to be recognized as a series of the greatest achievements of any people... anywhere. And driving them was most likely only one major impulse: to eventually be able to worship in a community setting.

"From our earliest beginnings of thought and desire, there had to be a desperate hoping. Most likely it was not clear how life was conceived; the marvel of conception was not fully appreciated for eons.   Nor was the effort simply to stay alive once life was brought forth and clearly understood; it took too much energy to just stay alive to give it anyone's full attention.   But what did impact each and every member of those earliest of pioneers was the devastating effect of the death of their group or tribal members.   Death of relatives and remembrance of ancestors haunted our early relatives… and still does, if we are honest with ourselves.

"The reaction to death and how to remember those lost took on a visible and lasting significance by how these ancient peoples 'buried' their ancestors. Some did so by placing them above ground in particularly sacred places and let the wild animals consume them.   Eventually, family and tribal members would return and place the remaining bones in special places throughout their homeland.   Other members of these hunter/gatherer bands honored their departed loved ones through the practice of 'sky burials', where the deceased were laid to rest on elevated wooden platforms for vultures, and the like, to consume them.   Both these rituals gave rise to imbuing the respective surroundings of these earliest 'worshippers' with an everlasting connectedness and remembrance of their ancestors

"The earliest permanently constructed monument, which formalized these practices was found in Göbekli Tepe, Turkey.   It was dated as having been built 11,500 years ago. At this place there are multiple circular sites; their circumference defined by upright, stone pillars. Remarkably, they actually signify the first temples ever erected by our ancestors.   Some 2,000 years later at Çatalhöyük, Turkey, where the world's first city was excavated, this same ancestral reverence was still being practiced through the burial of family members' bones under the floors of their homes. This practice, too, gave a succeeding generation a stronger connection with their ancestors.

"This theme of ancestor worship and its accompanying desire to bury their dead in ways that kept them close by was to be complemented with another hunter/gatherer form of devotion. It was animism, the belief that common objects in nature, e.g. trees, animals, birds, even mountains, have souls or are manifestations of spirits. Both these observances led to a slow but steady consciousness of Something or Someone Greater, more pervasive that could or would communicate with these earliest humans.

"Together, these two belief systems, if you will, formed what was to evolve into the rudiments of religion, now with all its formalized traditions, observations, rituals and commandments.

"But I want to stop here and come back to this present moment in humanity's trek through time and beliefs to finish examining why it appears that this alien invasion, with all its devastation, befell us. It requires we back up to around 10,000 years ago, when the agriculture and domestication began for the first time in human history.

"In what has been described as a sparsely populated world of only thousands of individuals some 70,000 years ago grew to millions of human beings 10,000 years ago, to more than 6 billion today. The mushrooming of so-called civilized humanity led us to relocate primarily in cities around the world. And during this explosion of population there arose towns, cities and countries that were better at planting and harvesting foodstuffs. This, in turn, gave rise to governments, leaders, armies and the invariable consequence of wars and conquests.

"What had been a lifestyle entirely devoted to that of sacrifice and survival for hunter/gatherers, as odd as they seem to us now, evolved into one of warring to establish security and rampant greediness to insure comfort and status for city dwellers and their leaders. The seeds planted in those earliest days around 10,000 years ago had both a tangible and an intangible effect. In the former case, they gave the opportunity for many more to have an abundant life; and in the latter, they contributed significantly towards greater struggles that have seen no end, even to this very night.

"Everyone wanted more of something, be it property, treasure, sustenance, water, gold or the conversion of others to their way... the only way. No one, it seemed, was satisfied with less. Having to have or wanting more became insatiable appetites. And as far as I can tell, it was this unstoppable obsession that led to the scent of death, even though the actual full collapse of our societies had not begun unchecked, that brought Finality, who towers behind me on this stage, and her associates who surround us now, and have been responsible for the loss of hundreds of millions of our citizens here and throughout our world.

"It was as if those early nomadic people, with their pillars and etchings of vultures had some premonition of what we are now facing. Was there some visitation by these beings in those earlier times? I have been informed by Finality that there were. But something that our early ancestors began doing discouraged them from advancing further into our world. And I believe it was our earliest ancestors' deep desire and drive to worship... faithfully, fearlessly and without reservation.

"And that leads me to the second part of this

presentation tonight: what constitutes true worship and why wasn't whatever form that so many of us tried to practice enough to prevent what has happened? In other words, what is missing? What was it about the drive or urge to worship that began to fade, if in fact it is this reverential observance that I am supposing will save us from our final demise as a civilization?

"To begin with, we must understand what worship meant to those earliest practitioners. Worship by its very name means to give worth to something. It becomes apparent that doing so meant so much to our ancestors that they gave profound worth to whatever it was that they were honoring. It became an integral part of their daily lives. They became duty-bound not to forget, and in time they continually remembered to practice it. From individual praying, the simplest act of worship, to when the first temple was built in Göbekli Tepe, their daily lives were filled with the need and desire to formalize their gravest and most important convictions about the heavens and mortality, even in a communal setting.

"Finality and her wicked host of vultures became impressed enough with this surprising, life-sustaining process and how it somehow diminished the death spiral they sensed earlier being emitted from our earliest ancestors, that they were diverted away from our world. They were spared then what has now occurred to us over this last month.

"Why then did they return? What happened?

"I can only think that the civilization, which arose in mass over 10,000 years ago, developed the unrelenting process of accumulating goods, food, security, wealth for some and not for others and the undeterred ambition and irrational need to conquer and terrorize others caused enough of us to forget our origins.   Rather than remember, enough of us began to forget, deny and distort the worth, value and beauty of a simpler, awe-filled life;   one that took a humble delight in the astounding wonder of each day and an overpowering love that is always ours if we only truly worship.

"But let me stop here a moment and recognize that, indeed, there were those among you gathered here, and certainly among the countless number of those lost before this night who did worship faithfully and in truth.   There is no fairness when death arrives at one's doorsteps.   It sweeps all away with it.   All I can conclude is that there were not enough of us, me included, who did not understand the meaning of sincere and dedicated worship.   And some of us non-worshippers even escaped to this day the wrath of our invaders.   And I sincerely apologize to those of you who observed and worshipped so faithfully and have lost so much.   I am the least among you.   I turned away long ago from a life of worship.   It was due to circumstances far beyond my ability to understand that brought me to this place and time.   But you must understand that what I am saying this night, while coming from someone who was an apostate, must be heard and practiced.   The form towering behind me would not have allowed me to speak and say what I have up until now if it were otherwise.   Do not confuse the messenger with the message.   What I say is important... not me.   Not in any way.

"And know it is not enough to reverse the process of being a culture of irrational, even sinful, consumptive people.   We must not only learn to want and think we need less and less, but we must again humble ourselves and cultivate an indwelling spirit of daily worship.   And that leads me to the final words I have this night for you.   What

199

exactly is this worshipping that you and I must do?

"In private and in communion with others, worship, to be true and ever-transforming, must express joy and hope. It must be a refuge of safety, comfort and peace. It must recognize that we are not self-sufficient; that it is an act of both giving and receiving. We must learn how to honestly and gratefully do both. It must confirm by its observance that there is value in life; that it is not meaningless. It is no accident that you and I are here at this moment. And most of all worship anticipates and embraces the future, one filled with infinite goodness.

"Whatever, Whoever, however you worship, it MUST include a love of Some Being who is beyond yourselves, who engenders an all-encompassing love... of you and of all others. It must include an absolute imperative to avoid violence of any sort, whether by the senseless accumulation of possessions or by committing physical or emotional trauma. No true worship denies others the right to do so in a different way, as long as it promotes a loving tenderness for all. Period.

"It IS that basic and fundamental. Do your utmost to honor and be in the presence of the Holy and do your utmost to be aware of others around you. Strive to become someone who worships in private and in communion with others in countless ways, acknowledging we are not perfect creatures but ones always wanting to love and to be hopeful.

"Finally, you must not only practice what I have described in the briefest terms; but each of you must now sweep out from this place and tell everyone who you meet to do the same. Walk, run, drive, sail, fly... cover the world with this message. It is our only hope to have this horrible fate that befell us to leave and never return.

"And from those of us assembled here on this stage,

we offer you this simplest of worshipful prayers: 'May God be with you now and forevermore'."

Having said all this, I turned away from the lectern to see that Finality, in all her hulking presence, had disappeared. Puzzled, I then turned and faced the audience and stared out into its perimeter; there was no blackened border surrounding them. The 'stains' had also disappeared! I then turned back to President Franklin, Colleen and Tom and shouted, "THEY'VE LEFT !!! WE'RE ALONE !!"

And then the entire audience, to an individual began to shout, cheer, whistle and sing. The sounds of music filled the night! It was the beginning of a night that no one could adequately describe thereafter. We had been given a second chance at life. We had replaced a well-deserved vulnerability with hope and a future.

EPILOGUE

NINETEEN: STARTING ANEW

Most of the events that followed our departure from Sacramento, some of which are now being recorded elsewhere, were predictable. President Franklin bid Tom, Colleen and I a rather emotional farewell. Oddly, when you are enveloped in some event as staggeringly overwhelming as the one we witnessed over the last three weeks, you become closer, but in a desperate attempt to try and move on, you begin to set aside as many memories as you can. We had many to forget… each of us. That said, our farewells were not overly emotional. It was more relief. I thought that maybe in the years that followed we might remember one another in a more serene light.

It was good, however, to see President Franklin begin to restore her self-confidence and a sense of mission. What had happened to each of us in these last week's took a toll far beyond what any medical practitioner could sooth or medication could block. We were survivors of a terrifying war that we lost. But now it was time to rebuild.

I have been told since the departure of Finality and her legions and my reestablishing a home, of sorts, that when the President returned to Washington, D.C., the United States was to become a much, much smaller governmental entity. Rather than fifty states to preside over, President Franklin only had twenty-one. Many of the smaller eastern seaboard states merged, as did the Midwest and Southern states. Alaska and Hawaii, because of the distances and lack of communication, became territories again. It was only the larger Western states that retained most of their original borders, with the one exception of northern California and southern Oregon uniting to become the State of Jefferson, our twenty-first State, and the one I now live in.

Colleen and Tom bid me a temporary good-bye. They wanted to return to their home in the Palm Springs area and get whatever possessions they could use and prized. Amazingly, their daughter and son survived "The Consumption" and were in the Sacramento Airport audience that final night. Together they all drove back to Palm Springs and then up to where I now live. It was a great relief to me knowing that they were also settling where I would be heading.

And most remarkable of all, the entire remaining crew of Air Force One decided to fly back to where I drove to, once I left Sacramento. The country no longer had a need for two Air Force One's. And the President said, as a payment for their dedication and bravery, our crew could take our plane to Oregon. They were advised to simply keep it protected and in running order.

And finally, there was my plan. After hearing Finality describe the Paisley, Oregon area, in which the first humans made their initial settlement in the western hemisphere, I decided that was where I wanted to resettle. When my family and I lived in Oregon, we had visited the area a few times in the past. And I knew about the dry climate, availability of irrigation and tall mountains protecting the area from the strong northwestern storms. It seemed ideal to me, as it did to those first settlers.

And so, over the weeks and months that followed our crew came back together… even President Franklin did once her term of office expired.

That left only one other member of our flight. And one day, about two years after the stains and Finality disappeared so suddenly from Sacramento, there was a gentle knock at the front door of my modest home. I never locked it; there was no need to. All our neighbors were folks that were well known to me by that time. And there were very few visitors that came through the area. Everyone stayed put for years following this tragedy.

So I just called out from the table I was beginning to write this account on, "Come in! The door is open."

For no particular reason, I turned and looked towards it, primarily due to the slowness that it was being pushed open. Then, in the full light of the early morning sun, with the doorway framing her, there stood Finality. She was dressed differently, not in the stylish business suit that I always saw her wearing. Due to the rising high desert summer heat, she was wearing light-weight, casual work clothes. Overall, her appearance was still relatively youthful. She had lost the beleaguered and overly exhausted appearance that I last saw in Sacramento.

And then she spoke.

"Do you have the need for another farm or ranch hand? I was in the area and no longer have a home elsewhere. Nor is there anyone who will let me stay with them. I hoped you might. I mean you or anyone else, no harm... now or ever again."

My mouth dropped open, and I was speechless for

the longest time, as she stood there waiting for my reply. Finally, I summoned up the strength and will to speak, and replied, "...sure, we can always use a helping hand. Come in. But we have a lot to discuss before your workday begins."

APPENDIX

1. Air Force One's Flight Schedule:

    -Four Stopovers per Day:
    -May 15th:-Bangor Int'l Airport: Bangor, Maine.
                -Edward F. Knapp State Airport:
                    Montpelier, Vermont.
                -Concord Municipal Airport: Concord,
                    New Hampshire.
                -Westover Air Reserve Base:
                    Springfield, Massachusetts.
    -May 16th:-North Central State Airport:
                    Providence, Rhode Island.
                -Albany Int'l Airport: Albany: New
                    York.
                -Groton-New London Airport: New
                    London, Connecticut.
                -Harrisburg Int'l Airport: Harrisburg,
                    Pennsylvania.
    -May 17th: -Capital City Airport: Frankfort,
                    Kentucky.
                -John C. Tune Airport: Nashville,
                    Tennessee.
                -Yeager Airport: Charleston, West
                    Virginia.
                -Richmond Int'l Airport: Richmond,
                    Virginia.
    -May 18th: -Dover Air Force Base: Dover,
                    Delaware.
                -McGuire Air Force Base:
                    Wrightstown, New Jersey.
                -Port Columbus Int'l Airport:

Columbus, Ohio.

-Frederick Municipal Airport: Frederick, Maryland.

-May 19th:-Pope Air Force Base: Fayetteville, North Carolina.

-Columbia Metro Airport: Columbia, South Carolina.

-Fort Benning Army Base: Columbus, Georgia.

-Pensacola Naval Air Station: Pensacola, Florida.

-Three Stopovers per Day:

-May 20th: -Jackson Int'l Airport: Jackson, Mississippi.

-Birmingham Int'l Airport: Birmingham, Alabama.

-Polk Field-Fork Polk Army Base: Leesville, Louisiana.

-May 21st: -Robert Gray Army Airfield: Killeen, Texas.

-Tinker Air Force Base Oklahoma City, Oklahoma.

-Adam's Field: Little Rock, Arkansas.

-May 22nd: -McConnell Air Force Base: Wichita, Kansas.

-Jefferson City Memorial Airport: Jefferson City, Missouri.

-Des Moines Int'l Airport: Des Moines, Iowa.

-May 23rd: -Illinois Air Nat'l Guard Field: Springfield, Illinois.

-Indianapolis Int'l Airport:

Indianapolis, Indiana.
-Capital City Airport: Lansing, Michigan.
-May 24th: -Traux Field: Madison, Wisconsin.
  -Minneapolis-St. Paul Int'l Airport: Minneapolis-St. Paul, Minnesota.
  -Bismarck Municipal Airport: Bismarck, North Dakota.
-May 25th: -Pierre Regional Airport: Pierre, South Dakota.
  -North Platte Regional Airport: North Platte, Nebraska.
  -Schriever Air Force Base: Colorado Springs, Colorado.
-May 26th: -Albuquerque Int'l Airport: Albuquerque, New Mexico.
  -Luke Air Force Base: Phoenix, Arizona.
  -Nellis Air Force Base: Las Vegas, Nevada.
-May 27th: -Salt Lake City Int'l Airport: Salt Lake City, Utah.
  -Great Falls Int'l Airport: Great Falls, Montana.
  -Natroma County Int'l Airport: Casper, Wyoming.
-May 28th: -Mountain Home Air Force Base: Mountain Home, Idaho.
  -Joint Base Lewis-McCord: Tacoma, Washington.
  -Eugene Airport: Eugene, Oregon.
-May 29th:-Elmendorf Air Force Base: Anchorage, Alaska.

-Honolulu Int'l Airport: Honolulu, Hawaii.
-Sacramento Int'l Airport: Sacramento, California (late at night).

2. White House Complex:

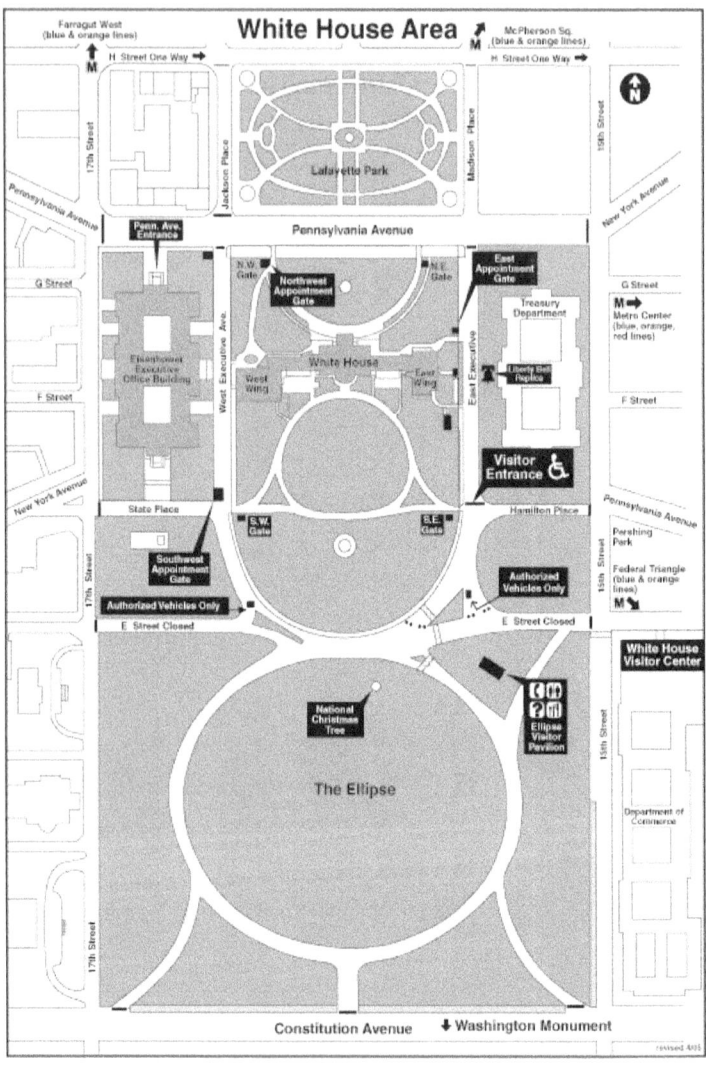

[1] Public Domain, courtesy of the Web Development Team within President Clinton's Whitehouse Staff.

3. White House West Wing Floor Plan:

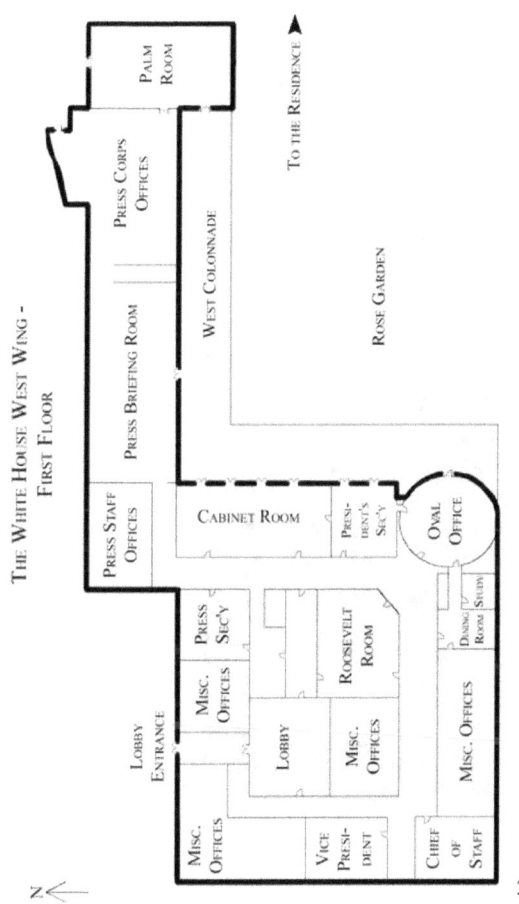

The White House West Wing - First Floor

- Palm Room
- Press Corps Offices
- To the Residence
- Press Briefing Room
- West Colonnade
- Rose Garden
- Press Staff Offices
- Cabinet Room
- President's Sec'y
- Oval Office
- Press Sec'y
- Misc. Offices
- Roosevelt Room
- Dining Room / Study
- Lobby
- Misc. Offices
- Misc. Offices
- Lobby Entrance
- Misc. Offices
- Vice President
- Chief of Staff

2

[2] Public Domain, courtesy of its author, Sarfa. Taken from Wikipedia.

4. The White House's Palm Room:

³ Public Domain, from the "Site Map of the White House Museum", found at www.whitehousemuseum.org.

5. Air Force One Flying Over Mt. Rushmore:

[4] Public Domain.   The image taken by a U.S. Air Force Airman or employee.   Taken from Wikipedia.

6. Paisley, Oregon Map:

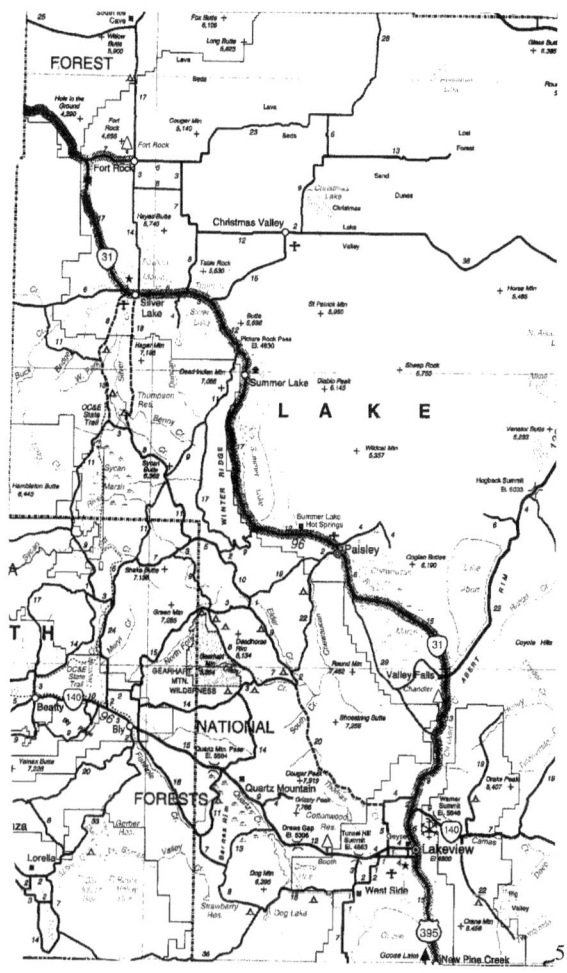

7. Last Glacial Maximum Map:

[5] Used with permission and courtesy of Oregon Department of
Transportation, 2009-2011 Official State Map.

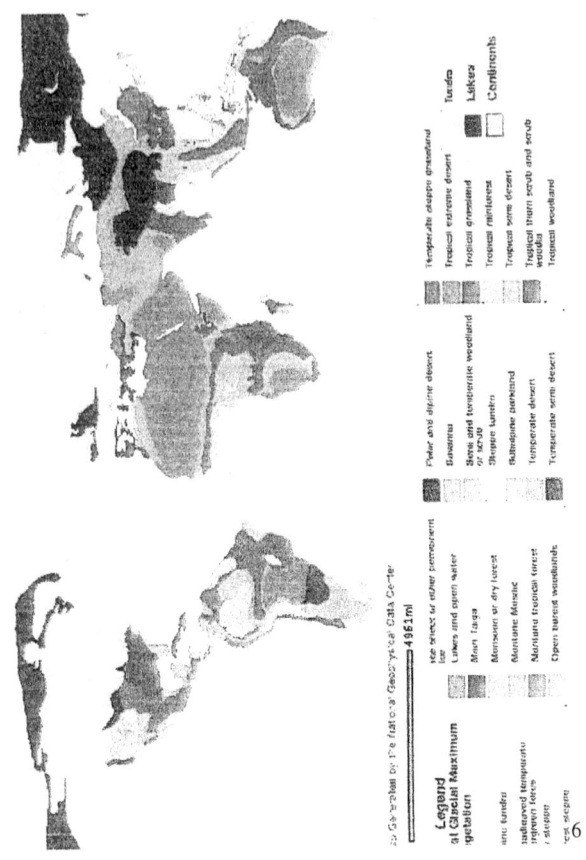

As Generated by the National GeoPhysical Data Center

4961ml

Legend
al Glacial Maximum vegetation

- Ice sheet or either permanent ice
- Lakes and open water
- Main Taiga
- Monsoon or dry forest
- Montane Mosaic
- Montane tropical forest
- Open burned woodlands
- Polar and alpine desert
- Savanna
- Semi and temperate woodland or scrub
- Steppe tundra
- Subtropical parkland
- Temperate desert
- Temperate semi desert
- Temperate steppe grassland
- Tropical extreme desert
- Tropical grassland
- Tropical rainforest
- Tropical semi desert
- Tropical thorn scrub and scrub woods
- Tropical woodland

Tundra
Lakes
Continents

alau tundra

Broadleaved temperate evergreen forest

al steppe

[6]

8. Map Site of Göbekli Tepe, Turkey:

---

[6] Public Domain.   Image created by employee of the U.S. National Oceanic and Atmospheric Administration.   Taken from Wikipedia.

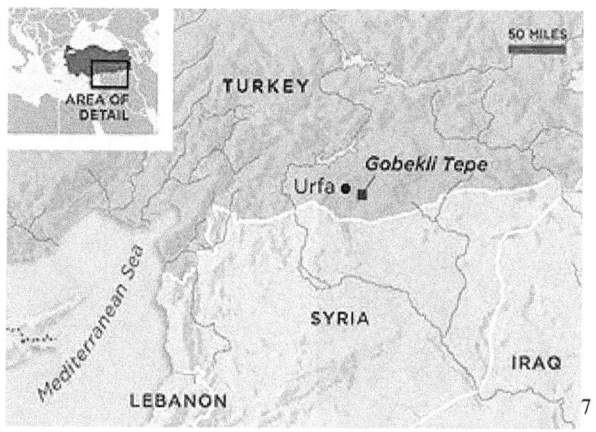

9. Pillar at Göbekli Tepe Representing Outstretched Arms:

8

10. Pillar at Göbekli Tepe with Images of Vultures:

9

REFERENCES

[9] © permission granted by Berthold Steinhilber, the photographer. Taken from Wikipedia.

1.   Pandora's Seed-The Unforeseen Cost of Civilization, Spencer Wells. Random House, New York, 2010.

2.   The Journey of Man, Spencer Wells. Random House Trade Paperback, New York, 2003.

3.   Confessions, Books I-VIII, St. Augustine. Great Books Foundation, Henry Regnery Co., Chicago, 1948.

4.   An Essay On Man- An Introduction to a Philosophy of Human Culture, Ernst Cassirer. Doubleday Anchor Books, Garden City, New York, 1944.

5.   The Little Flowers of St. Francis, St. Francis. E.P. Dutton and Co, Inc., New York, 1951.

6   The Idea of the Holy, Rudolf Otto. Oxford University Press, New York, 1950.

7.   For the Life of the World, Alexander Schmemann. National Student Christian Federation, New York, 1963.

8.   The Mystical Theology of the Eastern Church, Vladimir Lossky.   James Clarke & Co. LTD, London, 1957.

9.   The Byzantine Liturgy-A New English Translation of the Liturgies of St. John Chrysostom and St. Basil the Great, Russian Center. Fordham University, New York, 1956.

10.   Introduction to Liturgical Theology, Alexander Schmemann.   The American Orthodox Press, Portland, Maine, 1966.

11.   Ancient-Future Worship-Proclaiming and Enacting God's Narrative, Robert E. Webber. Baker Books, Grand Rapids, Michigan, 2008.

12.   A History of the Early Church, Hans Lietzmann. The World Publishing Co., New York, 1961.

13.   The Purpose of Man-Designed to Worship, A.W. Tozer. Regal Publishers, Ventura, California, 2009.

14.   World Religions from Ancient History to the Present, Geoffrey Parrinder, editor.   Facts On File Publications, New York, 1971.

15.   Neuroscience Concepts, Evaluation and Treatment-Applications in Traumatic Brain Injury, Josephine C. Moore, PhD., OTR. Lecture series January 20-22, 1995, San Francisco, California.

16.   Wikipedia, The Free Encyclopedia: Göbekli Tepe, Paisley Caves, Worship, Stages of Sleep, REM, Last Glacial Maximum, White House West Wing, White House Complex, Air Force One, Dreams.

17.   "The Hidden Brain-What Scientists Can Learn From Nothing," Sharon Begley. Newsweek, June 7, 2010, p. 24.

18.   "History in the Remaking-A Temple Complex in Turkey That Predates Even the Pyramids Is Rewriting the Story of Human Evolution," Patrick Synmes. Newsweek, March 1, 2010, pp. 46-48.

19.   "A Default Mode of Brain Function," Marcus E. Riaichle, et. al., PNAS , January 16, 2001, vol. 98, no. 2, pp. 676-682.

20.   "The World's First Temple," Sandra Scham. Archaeology , vol. 61, no. 6, Nov/Dec. 2008.

21.   Desiring the Kingdom-Worship, Worldview and Cultural Formation, James K.A. Smith. Baker Publishing Group, Grand Rapids, Michigan, 2009.

22.   Ancient-Future Worship-Proclaiming and Enacting God's Narrative, Robert E. Webber. Baker Books, Grand Rapids, Michigan, 2008.

23.   Worship: Reformed According to Scripture, Hughes Oliphant Old. Westminster John Knox Press, Louisville, Kentucky, 2002.

24.   The Beginnings of Religion, E.O. James. Greenwood Press, Westport, Connecticut, 1950.

25.   Generations of Praise-The History of Worship, Bruce E. Shields and David A. Butzu. College Press Publishing Co., Joplin, Missouri, 2006.

26. Private Worship, Public Values and Religious Change in Late Antiquity, Kim Bowers. Cambridge University Press, New York, 2008.

27. Real Worship-Playground, Battleground, Holy Ground?, 2nd ed., Warren W. Wiersbe. Baker Books, Grand Rapids, Michigan, 2000.

28. The New Golden Bough, James G. Frazer. S.G. Phillips, Inc, New York, 1959.

29. "Philosophy, Theology, Palmism and 'Secular Christianity'," John Meyendorff. St. Vladimir's Seminary Quarterly, St. Vladimir's Orthodox Theological Seminary, Crestwood, New York, vol. 10, no.4, 1966.

30. "Mystical Experience in the New Testament," Nicholas S. Arseniev. St. Vladimir's Seminary Quarterly, St. Vladimir's Orthodox Theological Seminary, Crestwood, New York, vol. 11, no. 1, 1967.

31. "The Glory of God in the Liturgies of the Christian East," Nicholas S. Arseniev. St. Vladimir's Seminary Quarterly, St. Vladimir's Orthodox Theological Seminary, Crestwood, New York, vol. 9, no.3, 1965.